Circle
of Light

Eliane Corbeil Roe

Circle
of Light

HARPER & ROW, PUBLISHERS,   New York
Grand Rapids, Philadelphia, St. Louis, San Francisco,
London, Singapore, Sydney, Tokyo, Toronto

Circle of Light
Copyright © 1989 by Eliane Corbeil Roe
Typography by Joyce Hopkins
1 2 3 4 5 6 7 8 9 10
First Edition

Library of Congress Cataloging-in-Publication Data
Roe, Eliane Corbeil.
   Circle of light / Eliane Corbeil Roe.
      p.   cm.
   Summary: When Lucy, a French-Canadian girl, allows herself to be talked into representing her school's eighth grade in a scholarship competition, she is surprised by the changes in others' attitudes toward her as well as by her own inner strengths.
   ISBN 0-06-025072-0 : $. — ISBN 0-06-025079-8 (lib. bdg.) : $
   [1. Schools—Fiction.   2. Examinations—Fiction.]   I. Title.
PZ7.R6215Ci 1989   89-45855
[Fic]—dc19   CIP
                                                               AC

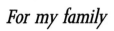

For my family

Circle
of Light

1

FROM HER DESK on the window aisle Lucy had been watching the clock on the front wall of the empty classroom. At a quarter past four exactly, the bell in Saint Margaret's church steeple released a solitary "Bong . . ." into the dark winter sky. Today was the third time she'd had to stay after school to "discuss" the scholarship competition with Sister Andrew. It would also be the last, because this time Lucy was determined to convince her teacher that she wasn't going to enter.

The rest of Lucy's class would have left the

3

school yard by now, but she could tell from the distant shouting that some of the boys had stayed to shovel the snow from the skating rink. Hoping Gabriel would be there, Lucy had decided to go out by the boys' door and walk past the rink.

At this hour nothing outside was visible, because the early darkness had transformed the window into a mirror. In the uneven, separate panes of glass the eighth-grade classroom became a huge picture puzzle with pieces that didn't quite fit together, with some parts repeated and other parts missing. Lucy could see her own broken-up reflection, a shadowy figure leaning forward, arms folded on top of her desk with row upon row of empty desks behind her, the round white ceiling lamps like full moons illuminating everything with the same cold light.

Lucy could also see Sister Andrew's reflection, sitting in the front row next to Laurence Constantine. It was probably because Sister Andrew had only been at Saint Margaret's since last September that she hadn't yet given up trying to help Laurence learn enough to graduate. Laurence was sixteen and as tall as a grown man. Lucy watched his wide shoulders straighten in the cramped chair desk and heard him say hesitatingly, "Eighty-one square feet?"

"That's correct!" Sister Andrew said, and gave

Laurence's paper such an enthusiastic tap with her pencil that the edge of her black veil fell over the sleeve of his checkered lumberjack shirt. The sight of the bright-red squares, dulled by the black filmy cloth, struck Lucy as unlucky, like walking on a grave.

Lucy drew her arms in close and shivered just as the school's front door, one floor down, slammed shut with such force that she felt the worn floorboards tremble beneath her feet. A moment later Yvonne and Mariette, the class monitors for the week, rushed into the room, laughing and pushing each other as they returned the cleaned blackboard erasers to their places along the ledge. With their squeaky whisperings they sounded exactly, it seemed to Lucy, like two mice.

Yvonne and Mariette's only remaining task was to water the pots of yellowed, spindly geranium plants on the windowsill. When they reached the plant closest to Lucy's desk, both girls turned at once and looked directly at her. Then they looked at each other, raising their eyebrows as if shocked at seeing the top student in the class being kept after school on the very first day after Christmas vacation.

Lucy closed her eyes. In a few minutes she too would be free to leave. She tried to picture

Gabriel—light-brown, curly hair and smiling brown eyes. He was the nicest-looking—and the nicest—boy Lucy had ever known. It had seemed unlikely from the first that he would ever notice her, with all the popular girls, like Madeleine Larose, crowding around him every day after school. But one day before the start of Christmas vacation Lucy had passed quickly by the group surrounding him and started the walk home from school by a shortcut she often used—a steep, rocky path from the school yard to the street in front of Saint Margaret's Church. And while she was climbing, someone called, "Lucy! Wait!" When she looked back, there was Gabriel hurrying to catch up.

"I'm on my way to the church to help Father Martin train the new altar boys for Christmas services," he explained as soon as they'd both reached the top. But Lucy was too overwhelmed to say anything. "Where are you going?" Gabriel asked after an awkward pause.

"Home," Lucy answered hoarsely.

Gabriel had climbed the steep path with Lucy almost every day until school closed for the Christmas holidays, even on days when there'd been no altarboy training, and even though he lived in the opposite direction. They'd stood by

6

the church steps afterward and talked before going their separate ways.

A loud noise broke through Lucy's reveries and made her eyes snap open. Laurence had stood up, raising the loose hinged seat, which had fallen back with a crash. "Thank you, Sister," he said, his deep voice echoing through the empty classroom. When he turned to leave, he noticed Lucy for the first time. By tomorrow Laurence and Yvonne and Mariette would have spread the news that they'd seen Lucy Delaroche still sitting at her desk after everyone else had gone. Gabriel would hear of it and wonder what she'd done.

To avoid Laurence's curious stare, Lucy watched Sister Andrew carry her chair back to the teacher's desk and take out the notebook she wrote in every day. "I'm not forgetting you, Lucy," she said. "Why don't you come over here?"

Lucy stood up resolutely, but by the time she reached Sister Andrew's desk, her knees were shaking. To calm herself, she followed the elegant loops and curves forming, as if by magic, under Sister Andrew's pen. Even reading upside down Lucy could tell that each letter was perfect.

Sister Andrew had replaced Sister Felicity, who had taught the eighth grade at Saint Margaret's longer than anyone could remember. Lucy was one of the few who had liked the new teacher from the very first. Almost everyone else in the class thought Sister Andrew made them work too hard. "She must think she's teaching at a university" had been the complaint.

But Lucy enjoyed Sister Andrew's lessons, which were sometimes confusing but always exciting, like challenging puzzles to be solved. Ever since Lucy had first learned to read, her older brother, Victor, had checked out books for her from the upstairs section of the Rockford Public Library, where children under twelve were not allowed to go. When Mama said she was worried that they were too difficult for someone Lucy's age, Victor told her, "Books that are too difficult are the best kind."

Lucy had started to look forward to coming to school—until the first time Sister Andrew asked her to stay after class and tried to persuade her to represent Saint Margaret's School in the province-wide scholarship competition. Lucy had refused and thought no more about it. But a few weeks later Sister Andrew had kept her after class again and asked her to reconsider. From that day on Lucy had grown afraid of Sister Andrew. She was so strong and sure of herself that she seemed, even more than the other nuns, to be living in another world, separate from ordinary people.

Sister Andrew closed the notebook and set it aside. She took off her glasses, polished them briskly with a corner of her veil, then put them back on. "You know, of course, why we're here," she said pleasantly.

"I don't want to compete for a scholarship," Lucy said, forcing herself to look straight into Sister Andrew's eyes. They were exactly the same blue-gray as Papa's.

Sister Andrew looked back calmly. "You thought over your decision during the Christmas vacation, as we agreed?"

"Yes, I did." Lucy's answer was firm, but what she'd really done, in fact, was to put the thought of this meeting with Sister Andrew out of her mind completely to keep it from ruining the holiday. "You'll have to ask somebody else," Lucy said.

She'd told Sister Andrew when they'd spoken before that she didn't stand a chance of winning. Even if, by some miracle, she did place first in the regional exams, it would be impossible to compete in the finals against other candidates from all over Ontario who had also placed first.

But Lucy couldn't tell Sister Andrew her most important reasons for refusing. The prize she'd be competing for was a four-year scholarship to a convent high school, and she didn't like being around nuns. Besides, if she had to stay after school to prepare for competition exams, she'd hardly ever see Gabriel outside class. Not even her two best friends, Claire and Alice, knew how much she looked forward all day to those few minutes with him near the steps of Saint Margaret's Church.

"What about Claire?" Lucy suggested desperately. "Claire is the one I'd choose."

"I thought you and Claire were close friends," Sister Andrew said.

"We are."

"Then you must know that there can be no question of asking Claire. She's had to miss too much school."

"It isn't fair! Claire loves school more than anybody!" Lucy objected. But she knew Sister Andrew was right. Claire was almost always behind in her schoolwork. As the oldest girl in her family, she'd had to stay home each time her mother was sick or had another baby. Some days there weren't enough shoes or coats for all the children in Claire's family to wear to school. "Claire should be the one to try for that scholarship," Lucy insisted. "She might win, too—she's very smart."

"Just the same, I'm asking you to agree to be Saint Margaret's first candidate," Sister Andrew said.

"Why me? There are all those others!" Lucy jerked her head backward at the rows of empty desks.

Sister Andrew leaned back and folded her hands in her lap. "I hope, Lucy," she said quietly, "that you're not fishing for compliments."

Angry tears rushed to Lucy's eyes. She blinked hard and looked down at the floor. It was gray with fine, chalky dust. With her head bowed down in silence, like someone pleading guilty, Lucy was sure that these endless discussions with Sister Andrew must be a punishment, probably for the sin of letting teachers believe mistakenly all these years that she was smarter than she really was.

Sister Andrew suddenly took hold of Lucy's hands. Startled, Lucy pulled back and felt Sister Andrew's cool, dry fingers tighten, then let go.

"Did you speak with your parents over the Christmas—?"

"With my mother," Lucy corrected brusquely. "My father died last year," she added, as if merely stating a fact.

"I'm . . . I'm very sorry. Was he . . . a war casualty?"

"No. He just died. At home. He was sick for a long time." The words snapped out briskly, but she had broken her own rule of never speaking to a nun about her family, especially about Papa, who almost never went to church and thought, like Lucy, that children should have regular teachers instead of nuns.

Sister Andrew stared down at her clasped hands, as if stunned.

"My brother Victor was a war casualty, though," Lucy said in a tense, mechanical voice. "He was wounded in the fighting, and died soon after, in an accident." Sister Andrew shook her head from side to side without looking up. "My cousin died too in the war," Lucy rushed on, "at the battle of Dieppe. A lot of French-Canadians died there. It's in France," she added quickly, remembering a rumor she'd heard, that Sister Andrew had been staying in a convent in Paris when the German soldiers marched into the city. "I did speak with my mother, though," Lucy said. It wasn't true, but she couldn't stop talking.

Sister Andrew's head came up sharply, and Lucy saw the white globe of a ceiling light flash, like a danger signal, across the flat round lenses of her glasses. "And what did your mother say?"

Lucy couldn't think of an answer.

"When you talked to your mother, what did she say?" Sister Andrew repeated.

"That I should do what I thought was best." The lie made Lucy's jaws so stiff that she could barely open her mouth. Still, she was sure that was what Mama would have said if she *had* talked to her.

"She leaves the decision entirely up to you, then?"

"Yes."

"And your answer is no."

"Yes. I mean it's no," Lucy said, trembling.

"You understand, don't you, Lucy, why I am asking you and not someone else?" Sister Andrew spoke quietly, but she seemed even stronger than before. "It's because in my judgment you have the best chance of winning. I'm not insisting like this just to torment you, and I'm not asking you to do this for me or for yourself. I'm asking you to do it for the honor of the school."

Lucy leaned back wearily on the desk behind her. Here it comes, she told herself. Except for Sister Andrew, all Lucy's teachers had told her that a superior intelligence was a special gift from God. One teacher had reminded Lucy that her older brother, Victor, who had also been at the head of his class while he was at Saint Margaret's, had received a similar special gift. When Lucy repeated to him what the nun had said, Victor had laughed as if at a very funny joke.

But Sister Andrew only said, "What we are given does not belong to us alone, to do with

13

exactly as we choose, to reject as we choose. Perhaps a community that allows such waste deserves to die out, as ours may."

Well let it, or let somebody else save it, Lucy thought. She had almost stopped breathing. Sister Andrew took both her hands again and gave them a little shake, as if to wake her up. "Will you do me a favor and think about this a little longer, until tomorrow? I promise never to mention the competition to you again if your answer is still the same."

"Yes," Lucy whispered, her eyes burning. This time she couldn't stop the tears. They squeezed out and rolled down her cheeks.

"We won't talk anymore today," Sister Andrew said. "Just go home, have your supper, and think it over one more time. Talk to your mother again if you like, and let me know tomorrow what you've decided." She gave Lucy's hands a last little shake, then released them.

Lucy carried her coat until she was safely outside the front door before stopping to put it on and fasten her boots. In the freezing darkness her fingers stiffened and fumbled. After searching her pockets in vain for a handkerchief, she rubbed her runny nose and wet cheeks hard with her wool cap. She started walking, pulling the cap hard onto her head until her ears were completely covered. Papa had always told her to wear her cap far down like this to keep warm, and Gabriel wasn't around now to see how stupid she looked with her head perfectly smooth and round as if it had been shaved, like a nun's.

It was much too quiet and lonely at this hour to go through the old cemetery behind Saint Margaret's Church as she'd started to do after talking with Gabriel. And it was too late and too dark to take the shortcut on the winding, frozen creek. The creek banks were steep and covered with tangled brush, so there was no way to leave the path until after it went through the culvert that tunneled under the railroad track not far from Lucy's house. The culvert was high enough to walk through, but it was long, and so dark inside at night that it was impossible to see anything except a pale circle of snow at either end.

She hated going home along the street because it meant passing Madeleine's house. Madeleine was not only the prettiest and most popular girl in Saint Margaret's, but also the one who came closest, after Lucy, to being at the head of the class.

Tomorrow, after Lucy had said no for the last time, Sister Andrew would ask Madeleine to represent Saint Margaret's in the scholarship competition. Madeleine's mother would probably buy her a whole new wardrobe. If Lucy had agreed to compete, she'd have continued to wear the three brown pleated tunics that were part of the uniforms her older sister, Tessa, had worn to convent school, each one exactly the same as the other two. Lucy's eyes and hair were a plain, medium brown that matched Tessa's old convent uniforms perfectly—unlike Madeleine's eyes, which were a deep, velvety brown.

Madeleine might even get the wristwatch she'd talked so much about last December, just before the midyear report cards. "My father promised me a gold watch for Christmas if I'm at the head of the class this time," Madeleine had told everybody. When the list was announced with Lucy's name in first place, as usual, Madeleine had burst into tears. Row after row, heads had turned to stare as she ran out of the classroom. Lucy had kept looking straight ahead, knowing the humiliation that Madeleine must be feeling, but not in the least sympathetic.

Once Madeleine was chosen to represent Saint Margaret's School in a scholarship competition, she'd be known not only as the prettiest and most popular girl in the eighth grade, but also as the smartest person in the entire school.

The street was empty and very still. Even the air looked frozen, and everything seemed far away except the stars. The stars really were far away, but their light was so sharp against the sky that they seemed to be hanging, like Christmas ornaments, just above the snow-covered roofs of the houses. The sudden shriek of a train whistle pierced the air as if the sound had come from the next street instead of miles away where the tracks followed the edge of the lake. Everyone in Lucy's family still looked up and smiled at each other whenever they heard a train whistle, as though it could still be Papa.

She was angry at herself for crying in front of Sister Andrew. She hadn't even cried at Papa's funeral, because she couldn't believe that he had died. She hadn't believed it until she saw the difference it made in everyday things. It would never again be Papa pulling the train's whistle chain and causing the sound that could be heard clear across a cold, dark winter night like this.

2

WHEN SHE CAME through the front door, Lucy smelled her favorite supper, fried steak and potatoes with plenty of onions, cooked until they were soft and caramelly. Supper was almost over, and Mama was pouring tea for Mr. Porter, their boarder. Tessa's twin babies hammered on their high chairs when they saw Lucy, knocking aside the spoonful of mashed potatoes their mother had been holding out to them. "Paul and Colette!" Tessa scolded, using both names to let them know she was angry. Most of the time everyone named the twins together, "Paul-ette."

18

Lucy squeezed into the chair next to her younger sister, Jeanie. "I set the table tonight, Lucy," Jeanie said. "It was your turn, so now you have to set it two nights in a row."

"Alice's mother called you," Edward chimed in before Jeanie had finished. "She wanted to be sure you were coming to help Alice with her French homework. She said she was afraid you might forget, since you didn't show up after school for your skating lesson. How Alice ever got into a French class, or into high school in the first place, is more than I can figure out."

Lucy had to let Edward's big-brother sarcasm pass this time. He was just jealous because Alice Palmer, probably the most glamorous and talented girl in all of Rockford, had become close friends with Lucy while ignoring him completely.

Lucy piled food onto her plate. Mama always fried the onions separately now, because Mr. Porter never ate them. Papa had always teased anyone who refused to eat onions, but he probably wouldn't have teased Mr. Porter, who worked in a bank and wore gray suits with vests, even to the supper table.

"You're late," Edward said. "I suppose you've been hanging around the skating rink at school to be with the boys?" Lucy said nothing and started eating.

19

"Why *are* you so late?" Mama asked.

"I had to stay after class to talk with Sister Andrew. She wanted me to represent Saint Margaret's in a scholarship competition." Lucy was surprised to see everyone stop talking to listen.

"What do you mean she 'wanted you to'?" Edward said.

"I hope it doesn't mean you refused?" Tessa asked. She was holding the spoon up very high, and the twins whimpered and tried to reach it even though they'd been refusing to eat a moment earlier. Lucy laughed, and so did Jeanie, but Mama, Edward, Tessa, and Mr. Porter all waited unsmilingly for Lucy to answer.

"Of course I refused," Lucy said. "I refuse every time, but she keeps asking me anyway. Tomorrow I'll tell her no for the last time, because she promised not to ask me again." Lucy looked at the solemn faces around the table. No one spoke. "The final prize is a scholarship to a convent high school. Even if I stood a chance of winning, there'd be no reason to do all that extra work for a prize I wouldn't accept in the first place."

Tessa's eyes flashed. "We already know your opinion of convent school. But this is . . . an honor! And you're turning it down?"

Lucy put her fork down. "Honor. That's what

20

Sister Andrew calls it. Is it supposed to be an honor to work harder than anybody else in school for something I don't want? I don't call that an honor. I call that stupid."

She'd been right not to mention the competition to anyone. She should have kept silent about it until *after* Sister Andrew had chosen Madeleine or, better yet, never spoken of it at all.

"I mean the honor of... of..." Tessa was making digging motions with the spoon, as if trying to dig the words she was looking for out of the air. Lucy laughed again.

"I don't see what there is to laugh about," Edward said. "*I* know what Tessa means even if Lucy doesn't. She means the honor of the Delaroche family, of all French-Canadians." Edward's face was flushed and tense. Mr. Porter was nodding in agreement.

Suddenly, Edward stood up and shoved his chair back, as if about to deliver a speech. He looked at Mama, who continued to sip her tea, then around the table at everyone except Lucy. "Lucy doesn't care about this family. What *Lucy* wants is all that matters to her!" Edward glared at Lucy across the table, then sat down. Lucy stared calmly back at him. "Isn't it about time you started thinking about the rest of the family?" he shouted.

Lucy stood up, pushing her chair back as Edward had done, except that hers tipped backward and hit the floor. At the loud noise both twins opened their mouths wide and started to cry at exactly the same time. This time everyone laughed except Lucy. She was already out of the kitchen and on her way up the stairs, which shook and creaked as she raced up, two steps at a time.

Edward had continued to shout after her, but Lucy couldn't tell what he was saying. At the landing she stopped. She had no place to go. The room she'd been sharing with Jeanie had become Tessa's while she waited for her husband to find a job and a place to live. Until that happened, Lucy was sleeping on a folding cot in the downstairs front hall.

"Why doesn't Lucy just admit that she's ashamed of her family?" This time Edward's voice reached her clearly.

Lucy ran up the last few steps. On her right was the door to the attic. She yanked it open and climbed the steep wooden steps. The attic was unheated, and when she reached the landing, she could see the pale cloud of her breath in the dim light from the window.

"I'm not ashamed," she said aloud. "And I'm not selfish." Her hands curled into fists. "Why aren't you ashamed, Edward?" she said, punching the cold air like a boxer. "Why aren't you ashamed of being in vocational school? Why are you training yourself to be a carpenter instead of a doctor or a lawyer, somebody who would bring honor to the family, if that's so important? It's too hard and it takes too long, that's why."

Lucy brought her hands together and blew on her fingers to warm them. "Let somebody else go to all that trouble," she whispered, shivering uncontrollably. Mama's cedar blanket chest stood under the landing window. Lucy sat down on it and tried not to think of her plate of hot, delicious supper. She couldn't go down yet, not while everyone was still sitting around the kitchen table. She curled her legs under for warmth and looked out.

If she'd ever claimed that the prizes she won in school every year were bringing honor to the family, everyone would have laughed. And Edward would probably have laughed hardest. Once, when a visitor had started to praise her and Victor for doing well in school, Papa had interrupted him. "All my children are smart," he said.

Papa wouldn't have allowed her to leave the table in that actressy way, like the heroine in a movie. She was sorry now that she'd left. For one thing, people in movies always had someplace to go to, like a garden or a room of their own. They never ended up freezing in a dismal attic, wishing they could go back and finish their supper. The attic smelled of old wood and dusty, closed-up air. Nobody came up here in the winter. Jeanie was sure there were ghosts.

She wished she were at Alice's house instead, in Alice's pretty bedroom, reading the advice columns aloud from the latest magazines or arguing over the pictures of clothes and hairstyles. The fact that Alice was a year older than Lucy and a first-year student at Rockford High School hadn't stopped them from becoming close friends, even though Alice's skating and dance lessons and practice kept her busy after school.

Lucy was sure that in a convent school she wouldn't have the chance to be friends with someone like Alice, or to have two friends who were as completely different from each other as Alice and Claire. Tessa and her friends had all come back from convent school exactly the same, pale and fat and silly around boys. That was probably why Tessa had married Leo without graduating, as soon as he was called into the army. She couldn't even wait until he came back.

"No convent school for me," Lucy said out loud. Next September Alice would be in her second year at Rockford High, and she'd promised to help Lucy find her way around at first. Best of all, for Lucy, would be having ordinary teachers instead of nuns.

Lucy's forehead started to ache. She leaned it against the cold glass and saw that a band of frost had formed on the lower inside edge like a tiny forest of white, lacy ferns. The attic door opened. Mama appeared in the rectangle of light from the hallway. "I put your plate in the oven," she said as she came up the stairs. She sat down opposite Lucy on the blanket chest.

"I'm sorry I didn't eat," Lucy said.

Mama shivered. "It's freezing up here." The silver streaks in her softly waved hair shone in the dim light of the window. "I hope you're warm enough at night," she said. "It isn't right for you to be sleeping in the front hall."

Lucy laughed. "Why isn't it? You and Jeanie are sleeping in the dining room, and Jeanie says she hasn't had any nightmares since she moved in with you."

"But are you getting enough sleep? There's so much noise with people going in and out. And the front door lets in the cold."

"I don't mind."

"Well, *I* mind. But there isn't much I can do

until Leo finds a job and sends for Tessa and the babies . . . . And then, of course, I'll miss them . . . ."

"You have so many other things to worry about," Lucy said. "Don't worry about me."

"I worry about all of you," Mama said in a low, firm voice.

Lucy breathed a circle of mist onto the cold glass and wrote her name in it. She drew the *y* into an elegant scroll of horizontal figure eights until she ran out of space, then wiped the glass clear with her hand. Their house was old-fashioned and taller than those around it. The window of the attic landing looked out onto the bare, rocky landscape that stretched for miles beyond the edge of town and now lay hidden under the snow.

"That competition does sound like a very hard thing to do," Mama said, breaking the silence. "But then everything you do in school seems hard to me. I wish I'd had more education so I could help you with your schoolwork the way parents are supposed to. . . ." Her words trailed off; then she said cheerfully, "So—your teacher picked *you* to represent the whole school?"

"Yes. But Sister Andrew made a mistake. I don't stand a chance of winning." Lucy stood up. "It's too cold up here. Let's go back."

But Mama didn't move.

"Tessa and Edward think it's such a big honor," Lucy said impatiently. "But it isn't." She took a step down from the landing, and went on speaking without turning around. "Saint Margaret's has the only eighth-grade class in this district, and Sister Andrew says all the other districts have two or more, which means they have more students to choose from. The other districts have also been taking part in this competition for years, so they've had a lot more practice."

"You think you don't have a chance?"

"I'm *sure* I don't."

"I thought you liked Sister Andrew. Haven't I heard you say that she seems to know everything? She may know something about you that you don't."

"Sister Andrew doesn't know *anything* about me," Lucy said. "*I* know what I can do and what I can't. I can't do this. And I don't want to."

Mama got up slowly. "Come and eat your supper," she said, giving the back of Lucy's neck a gentle push from behind. Her hand felt warm in spite of the cold.

The kitchen table had been cleared of everything except Lucy's knife and fork. Edward was at the sink washing the dishes and Jeanie was drying them. Edward turned around when Lucy came in and lifted his soapy, dripping hands out of the dishwater, as a sign that he was doing her job.

Lucy took her plate out of the oven. "So what are you going to do?" Edward asked. Lucy pushed the oven door shut carefully with one foot and sat down to eat. Edward had wiped the tabletop too fast and left wet streaks and crumbs. The onions along the edge of her plate had burned black. She picked up the shriveled pieces one by one with her fingers and ate them.

"Well, have you made up your mind?" Edward asked again. The front of his school shirt was stained with dishwater. Lucy stared at the wet spots until Edward was forced to look down at them too.

"What I've made up my mind to do right now," she said slowly, "is finish eating my supper."

It seemed now, for the first time, that it might be easier after all just to do what Sister Andrew wanted. She wouldn't have to argue anymore, not with Edward and Tessa, and especially not with Sister Andrew. And she wouldn't have to watch Madeleine become Saint Margaret's first candidate and be admired by everyone more than ever. Of course, no one would admire Lucy. If they noticed in the first place that she was competing for a scholarship, they'd make funny remarks, or pitying ones like "How can you stand all that extra studying? I'm sure glad it's you and not me."

Lucy looked at the remaining food on her plate and put down her fork. She wasn't hungry after all.

3

THE NEXT MORNING Lucy sat at the table long after she'd finished her breakfast, her hands wrapped around her empty cup, which was still warm from the hot cocoa. Next to her Jeanie's black cat, Min Min, lay sleeping, curled up in a patch of sunlight.

The radio had announced the weather report: The day would be bright and sunny but very cold, with dry, freezing winds. Lucy stroked the cat's glossy fur, which was hot from the sunshine. Min Min's green-yellow eyes opened, then closed again and disappeared in the blackness of his fur.

"I wish *I* could spend the day here, asleep and warm," she whispered to the cat. In a few minutes she'd have to go out in that freezing air and walk to school. She was determined to have her final talk with Sister Andrew as soon as she arrived instead of waiting and dreading it the whole day. Then she'd be free to go skating right after school. Gabriel would be at the rink too, she was sure.

Jeanie came into the kitchen from having her hair combed and braided by Mama. She was ready and anxious to leave for school, with her coat and snow boots on and her long wool scarf draped around her neck. Jeanie dangled the fringe of her scarf on top of Min Min's head. He opened his eyes and lifted one paw lazily toward the scarf.

"Why don't you leave him alone?" Lucy said. "Even a cat doesn't get to do what he wants in this house."

"He's *my* cat," Jeanie said, taking off her scarf and handing it to Lucy. On very cold days someone had to wind Jeanie's scarf carefully around her head, leaving only a narrow slit for her eyes. And because it was so cold today, Lucy would have to leave for school early to walk with Jeanie and make sure she kept her face covered. Otherwise Jeanie would arrive at school with dead-looking frozen patches on her cheeks.

31

*　　*　　*

Lucy had to walk facing into the wind, with Jeanie clutching her arm and walking slightly behind with her face pushed against Lucy's shoulder. Lucy's eyes were forced almost shut by the reflection of the sun on the snow, and by the gusts of wind that sent showers of ice crystals as sharp as needles into her face.

"I sure hope all this cold doesn't make my nose start to bleed," Jeanie shouted, her voice muffled by Lucy's coat sleeve.

"Don't think about it—then it won't happen!" Lucy shouted back.

Jeanie's nosebleeds were famous throughout Saint Margaret's School. The rivers of blood always started suddenly and had usually run down her chin and the front of her clothes by the time Lucy arrived.

"You should be used to it by now," Lucy said. "Try not to get so scared every time. I won't be there next year, remember. You'll have to go to Sister Rose."

"Oh, I hope I never have to!" Jeanie moaned, tightening her grip on Lucy's arm. "People will think I've done something very bad if I have to see the principal."

"Sister Rose isn't just the principal. She's the school nurse, and she was a real nurse before, in

32

a hospital. She can take care of you better than I can."

"No she can't. She'd probably do something that hurts, or send me home." Lucy felt Jeanie shudder, as if being sent home from school was the worst thing that could happen. "You always know what to do, Lucy. I want *you* to take care of me, not Sister Rose."

"But next year I'll be across town at Rockford High," Lucy said, not letting on how happy it made her feel just to say it.

"I'm not that scared of Sister Rose," Jeanie said. "I'm just scared I'll forget and call her 'Old Lima Bean' to her face. To her old bean face." She giggled and let go of Lucy's arm.

They'd reached the corner, halfway to school, where Claire and Lucy usually waited for each other to walk the rest of the way together. Claire hadn't come to school since more than two weeks before the Christmas vacation, and she wasn't at the corner today either.

"She's late," Jeanie said.

"No she's not. We're too early."

They waited for a few minutes, stamping their feet against the cold, then walked on. "Which is your best friend, Alice or Claire?" Jeanie asked.

"They're both my friends. I haven't got a best friend."

"*I* have," Jeanie said smugly.

"You have a different one every couple of weeks," Lucy said.

"Claire has those awful pimples. And she smells bad. Everybody says so. But Alice is so pretty!"

"Don't be such a ninny!" Lucy said angrily.

Jeanie had seen one of her classmates up ahead. As she ran to catch up, her scarf loosened and slipped from her face. She took her glasses from her pocket and put them on. "It's too cold to wear your glasses outside!" Lucy yelled after her, but her words were carried away on the wind and the blowing snow.

Jeanie had been delighted to learn that she needed glasses. "They'll make me look just like a teacher," she said. Lucy had laughed at Jeanie and teased her until Papa made her stop. Later on, when she saw Jeanie's eyes behind the thick lenses, swollen and watery-looking, Lucy had felt sorry for her. For once she hadn't needed Papa to prevent her from telling Jeanie exactly what she thought—that she looked like a fish staring out of a bowl, that only a fool would be glad to have bad eyesight, and that only an even bigger fool would want to look like a teacher.

Lucy had never criticized Claire's appearance, of course, although other people at Saint Margaret's made fun of the short, uneven haircuts her father gave her. It was true that the air inside Claire's house was always thick with a sour smell. Lucy had noticed it on her own clothes after she'd been there only an hour or two, but it was mean of Jeanie to say that she smelled bad.

In many ways, it seemed to Lucy, Claire was superior to everyone else at Saint Margaret's. For one thing she never complained except in a joking way, about having to work so hard at home and missing school. And even when she was sent home by the public health nurse for something catching, like lice or scabies, Claire always came back acting perfectly normal. Lucy would have been too embarrassed to come back at all.

Lucy looked back. There was still no sign of Claire. She'd probably be absent again today, but no matter how much school she missed, Claire always stayed in the same grade as Lucy and the rest of the class. That was partly because Lucy went to Claire's house to help her catch up on her schoolwork. But if Lucy entered the competition, she wouldn't have time to help Claire. Claire would understand why Lucy didn't want to take part in the competition. Today, more than ever, Lucy missed Claire and hoped she *would* show up at school.

At the edge of the school yard Lucy stopped

to watch Sister Isabel play circle tag with her first graders. She wanted to delay as long as possible before going inside to speak with Sister Andrew. The children in Sister Isabel's class had stamped the shape of a large wheel in the snow and were chasing each other wildly, trying not to step outside the spokes and rim. Sister Isabel had tucked her long skirt in at the waist to keep from tripping on the hem as she ran back and forth, dodging her pupils. Her feet and ankles, usually hidden, were graceful and pretty, even in the ugly black galoshes that all nuns wore in winter. The children were laughing and screaming with excitement. They seemed not at all surprised at how fast Sister Isabel could run and turn in spite of her heavy skirts.

Sister Isabel was only slightly taller than Lucy. She had perfect skin and soft gray eyes that she opened wide, as if with surprise, each time one of her pupils tagged her. On her arrival at Saint Margaret's two years ago there'd been much talk among the girls as to just how beautiful Sister Isabel would look dressed in ordinary clothes. Even some of the older boys had taken part in these discussions, but they admired Sister Isabel most of all because she'd won trophies for swimming and long-distance running. Every autumn and spring Sister Isabel was outside at recess, her veil pinned back, teaching her first graders the right way to pitch a baseball and swing a bat.

Someone shouted, "Jeanie's nose is bleeding again!" Lucy hurried toward the gathering crowd of girls. At its center she found Jeanie with her head bent forward over a bright-red stain in the snow. Calmly taking hold of Jeanie's shoulders, Lucy steered her in the direction of the school entrance, followed by the others. As they walked, Lucy reached inside Jeanie's coat pocket, took out her handkerchief, and pressed it under Jeanie's nose. Jeanie kept her head down and let herself be moved along like a rag doll, which always frightened Lucy more than the blood, down the basement stairs.

The girls' bathroom was dim and narrow, and smelled of strong disinfectant. Today it also smelled of cigarette smoke. Lucy heard the rattle of a toilet handle and a rush of water just as she and Jeanie reached the doorway. Yvonne and two seventh-grade girls Lucy didn't know were standing at the far end of the room. They watched Lucy prop Jeanie up in front of a basin.

Jeanie held tightly to the rim of the basin and tipped her head back as far as she could without falling. Her glasses had fogged over from coming indoors. They made the top part of her face look blank and empty, like an eyeless mask, above her blood-streaked nose and chin.

Lucy folded a wad of toilet paper and soaked it in cold tap water. She placed it over Jeanie's nose and held Jeanie's head so that she could lean back farther. Jeanie moaned. "I hate it when the blood leaks down my throat like this!"

Lucy's stomach heaved. "Don't talk!" she said, her voice thick. Even though it was too soon to check, she lifted the wad of paper. Attached to it was a quivering mass, like bright-red jelly.

"What's happening?!" Jeanie screamed, and pulled her head up. Her glasses were clear now, and she saw herself in the mirror above the basin. "My inside is coming out. My whole inside is coming out!" Jeanie's hands flew up wildly toward her face and knocked her glasses crashing against the wall. Then her eyes closed and she sank toward the floor.

Yvonne rushed forward and caught Jeanie, breaking her fall. The other girls stood even farther back and stared in fright as Yvonne brushed the hair back from Jeanie's face. "Geez! Lucy!" Yvonne whispered. "She's white as a sheet!" But Jeanie's face wasn't white. It was bluish gray, and looked dead. Nothing like this had ever happened before. Lucy dropped to her knees and tried to hold Jeanie's head up, but it slipped through her hands and fell back with a hard bump onto the cement.

"Do you want me to get Old Lima Bean?" one of the other girls offered just as the school bell rang. At the sound Jeanie's eyes popped open. "I'll be late for class!" she said, and scrambled to her feet. Lucy helped her while the three girls stared, as if witnessing a miracle. Yvonne picked up Jeanie's glasses, which had fallen under the basin, and placed them reverently in her hands.

Jeanie wiped the last streaks of blood from her face, then breathed on her glasses. She found a clean space on her red-stained handkerchief, polished the lenses with it, and put the glasses back on. Lucy held Jeanie's mittens under the faucet, until the ice-cold water ran clear of blood, then squeezed them as hard as she could. Her own hands were still weak and shaking.

Jeanie's round cheeks were almost their usual pink by the time she and Lucy had gone back up the stairs together. They stood by as the girls' lines filed past on their way to the classrooms. Jeanie slipped smoothly into her own place in line without a word or a backward look. Lucy took deep breaths of the cold air from the open doors and tried not to think of anything. When she sat down at her desk, she realized that she was still holding tightly on to Jeanie's wet mittens. She shook them out and placed them side by side on the sunny windowsill between two geranium pots.

When morning prayers began, Lucy lowered her eyes and saw that the edges of her fingernails were dark with dried blood. Then she remembered that she hadn't yet spoken to Sister Andrew, and the heated air of the classroom suddenly became hard to breathe. She wanted to lay her head on top of her desk and stay there all day without having to do anything, or hear or say anything. She especially wanted not to have to speak again with Sister Andrew, even though this time would be the very last.

Lucy went home for lunch and brought her skates to school. When the four-o'clock bell finally rang, she still wasn't ready to face Sister Andrew. She went out to the coatroom with the rest of the class, put her coat on, and hung her skates by their laces over her shoulder.

When she went back inside the classroom, Sister Andrew was at her desk writing something for Laurence, who turned to Lucy with a smile as she approached and stood next to him. Sister Andrew looked up. "These are an excellent idea," she said, pointing to Lucy's skates. "I understand that your day had a difficult beginning. You ought to have some fresh air before we talk. Why don't you come back in twenty minutes or so?"

Lucy went out by the school's front door, instead of the back as she'd meant to. She ought to have told Sister Andrew right away that her answer was still no. She didn't want to go back. What if Edward was right that it was selfish not to take this chance to do something that might make Mama proud? Victor wouldn't have hesitated for a second to enter this competition. The nuns who had taught Victor still spoke of him as Lucy's "brilliant" older brother. From the way their eyes shone when they said it, Lucy was reminded that "brilliant" also meant a kind of sparkling.

One of Lucy's clearest memories of Victor, since he had died, was the way he'd always tossed his books sideways onto the hall table, like a football, when he came home from school. Even after he'd started taking extra classes in high school, Victor had continued to do his schoolwork after supper at the kitchen table with everyone else. "Listen to this!" he'd say excitedly, then read aloud from something he was studying. It could be a poem or a passage from a geography or science book. There seemed to be nothing that Victor didn't find interesting and full of wonder.

41

Once *she'd* left Saint Margaret's, Lucy was certain, no one would ever use the word "brilliant" when speaking about her.

Lucy walked around to the back of the school and sat on a bench next to the rink. Putting on Tessa's old skates took a long time. The leather was soft, and she had to pull very hard on the laces to make them tight enough. The low rays of the setting sun had turned the air, the ice, and the skaters all the same brassy color. Some of the seventh- and eighth-grade boys were trying to play hockey, but she couldn't find Gabriel among the dodging, fast-moving players. Lucy stood for a while outside the rink, next to the entrance. Her feet were cold inside the tight skates, and her arms and legs felt like stone.

At the center of the ice, where there were fewer skaters, Madeleine was practicing arabesques and spins that made the pleats of her blue tartan skirt flare out in crisp arcs and circles. After almost two months of weekly lessons and hours of practice with Alice, Lucy was still very far from being able to perform the figures that Madeleine was moving through effortlessly. Like Alice, Madeleine could bend far over, as if trusting the empty air to support her. But Lucy couldn't make herself forget that the narrow, curved edge of a skate blade was her only contact with solid ground.

Lucy had just stepped onto the ice and was skating slowly along the edge when she suddenly felt a blow, like an explosion, under her feet. Her hands flew up and reached clumsily for the fence as both feet slid out from under her.

The hockey puck had shot across the ice, she realized after a moment, and struck her skate blade with full force. She was still clinging help-lessly to the scarred fence boards, trying to regain her footing, when someone yelled, "Watch out, Lucy!" She turned angrily, and saw Gabriel appear suddenly out of the noise and confusion. He was skating fast toward her carrying a hockey stick and seemed, in fact, about to run straight into her. Lucy braced herself against the fence. But at the very last moment Gabriel turned sideways and stopped only a few inches away in a shower of fine, scraped ice. With his free hand, still in its padded glove, he took Lucy's arm and supported it until she was standing.

Then Gabriel lowered his hockey stick, scooped the puck neatly from under Lucy's feet, and slammed it across the ice to the other players. He followed after it for a short distance, then spun around again toward Lucy and raised his hockey stick to his shoulder, like a soldier holding a rifle. Moving slowly backward, he touched his fore-head with the tip of his glove in a comic salute

43

that made her laugh. "Sorry, Lucy," he said, then turned and raced back to the game.

Lucy let go of the fence and started to skate. It had all happened in the space of a few seconds, yet a brightness radiated from someplace inside her. She felt weightless except for her arm, which could still feel the pressure where Gabriel's bulky glove had held it. And she could still see Gabriel's brown eyes, which had looked worried, as though he thought she might have been hurt, then smiling, as if the whole incident had been a secret joke between them.

Lucy skated faster and faster, dodging smoothly in and out among the other skaters. At the corner her right foot rose, as if by itself, crossing over the left in long, even glides. Without looking, she could tell exactly where Gabriel was by the red headband that flashed like a bright signal at the corner of her vision.

She smiled and whispered, "Relax, Lucy!"—the words Alice had yelled out to her again and again. For the first time, with the ice flowing past underneath her as naturally as the water in a river, Lucy understood what Alice meant. This was the way skating was supposed to feel, like being part of a river, like snow falling.

Lucy was still skating when the sun disappeared behind a bank of gold clouds on the horizon. The string of bare light bulbs above the rink blinked on, and under their glare the shadows moving against the ice surface were round and dark. The hockey game was over and the players were leaving. Gabriel had taken off his gloves and was carrying them in one hand as he skated slowly along, just ahead of Lucy.

Lucy had picked up speed and was skating almost parallel to Gabriel, on the outside, when she saw Madeleine move toward him in a wide, smooth circle from the center of the rink. "Skate with me, Gabe," Madeleine said, and took his arm. Gabriel let himself be pulled along, then threw his gloves over the fence and put his arm around Madeleine's waist.

At the next opening in the fence Lucy stumbled out onto the snow. By the time she'd changed out of her skates, Gabriel and Madeleine were moving faster than anyone else, so they had to break apart to let the slower skaters slip between them. At the corners they both leaned far over, lifting and crossing their feet at exactly the same time, as if they were one person.

By the time Lucy got back to the classroom, she'd been gone almost an hour. Sister Andrew was busily examining a shelf filled with books and papers. "I'll only be a moment," she told Lucy. Lucy went to her own desk and sat down. She'd secretly believed all these years, without admitting it even to herself, that she must be at least a little smarter than Madeleine. But it wasn't true after all. Madeleine had known that if she wanted to skate with Gabriel, all she had to do was ask.

"I'll do it," Lucy said loudly to Sister Andrew from the back of the room.

Sister Andrew turned around. "My dear child!" she said. Lucy had never heard Sister Andrew call anyone "dear," or even "child." But her own words had shocked her much more.

4

THE NUNS' STUDY was a small, boxlike room that seemed suspended dangerously, like a bird's cage, from the high ceiling of the second-floor corridor above the boys' stairs. A narrow, highly polished stairway led up to a door made of dark wood with a window of patterned glass that allowed only a broken, milky light to come through. The door was kept locked, as everyone knew from seeing the nuns open it with the key that each carried on a long black cord among the folds of her skirt.

No student had ever been allowed inside, as

far as Lucy knew, and it was generally believed among students at Saint Margaret's that the nuns' study was actually a bathroom. Lucy was grateful that no one was around to see her climb the polished stairs the next day, right after morning recess. She recognized the pattern in the window glass, of small stars or snowflakes crowded together. It was the kind of glass used in bathroom windows.

Even though Sister Andrew had sent her there to study, Lucy half expected to find the door locked, as usual, and was surprised to feel the knob turn smoothly and easily. The room was small, with plain white walls and a shiny wood floor, and furnished only with a square table which held a lamp and four chairs pushed under precisely, one to each side. They left barely enough space to get by the glass-fronted bookcases that lined the two side walls. A narrow window across the top of the far wall showed a strip of blue winter sky. It filled the room with bright, cold light. The chilly air was heavy with the smell of wax and varnish.

Lucy had set her books down on the table and was still standing just inside the room when she heard the door swing shut behind her. She turned in panic and tried the knob. To her relief, the door opened onto the empty corridor. Muted sounds floated up from the classrooms, a mixture of after-recess singing, praying, and recitation. No one suspected that she was standing there like a ghost, listening. Lucy stepped back inside and closed the door.

Shading her eyes with her hands, she peered through the glass of the nearest bookcase, then pulled one of the metal knobs. The glass panel slid upward and folded back, out of sight. The books looked as if no one had touched them for years. She'd taken old books like these from their shelves in remote corners of the Rockford Public Library, now that she was thirteen and allowed on the upper level. Their pages were so thin and dry that when she turned them, they left a fine powder on her fingers.

Beyond the bookshelves along one far wall, where Lucy hadn't noticed it at first, was a narrow door. It opened onto a tiny bathroom the size of a closet, with a toilet and a washbasin. The rumors were true, and the only difference between the nuns' bathroom and any other was its perfect cleanliness. A folded white hand towel, stiffly ironed, hung next to the basin. Even the white cake of soap was dry and smooth.

The only truly surprising object was the mirror above the sink. Nuns were not allowed to look in mirrors, not even to pin on their complicated headdresses and veils. When Lucy looked into the mirror, her own plain brown eyes gazed back, like the eyes of someone staring out of a prison window.

Lucy heard footsteps and the whisper of cloth outside the study door. She slipped quickly out of the bathroom, closed the door, and dropped into the nearest chair just as the study door opened. Sister Rose entered the room. Lucy stood up again. "Good morning, Sister," she said loudly, above the scraping of her chair.

Sister Rose tucked her hands inside her sleeves until the black cloth came together at her wrists. Although Lucy had seen nuns do this hundreds of times since, the gesture brought back vividly her fascination and terror on first seeing a nun who seemed to have no hands.

Sister Rose looked around the room. Her eyes stopped at the bookcase that Lucy had forgotten to close. Sister Rose's face really did look just like a lima bean, Lucy thought uneasily. It was impossible to tell if she was shocked at finding a student in the nuns' study, or if she was only making sure that Lucy disturbed nothing in this perfectly clean room. Sister Rose might even have come to use the bathroom!

But Sister Rose pulled the glass door back into place, then stood across the table from Lucy.

"Please sit down, Lucy," she said. Lucy sat down and crossed her hands on top of the book Sister Andrew had given her to begin her studies. Sister Rose bent forward. "What's wrong with your hands?"

"Nothing." Lucy's hands had been chapped all winter, as usual, and she paid no attention to the thick, darkened skin that made them look as if they hadn't been washed in a long time.

Sister Rose clicked her tongue—in disapproval, Lucy thought through the uncomfortable silence that followed until Sister Rose remarked, this time with unmistakable kindness, "That must make writing somewhat painful."

"I'm used to it," Lucy said with a nervous, crooked smile, and moved her hands down to her lap under the table.

"I'll bring you some cream to put on them. It's very good. It's the kind used in hospitals to prevent bedsores."

Lucy shivered.

"You're cold," said Sister Rose. "And I'm forgetting that I came to show you how to turn on the heat. This room is not usually heated."

Sister Rose turned the valve of a small radiator that stood against the wall under the window. "Come and warm those poor hands for a moment before you begin to work." When Lucy placed her hands next to Sister Rose's on the warming metal, she realized how stiff and cold she'd felt from the moment she'd entered the nuns' study. The thought of spending hours every day alone in such a dismal, cell-like room was suddenly more than she could bear. She lifted her hands from the radiator and clasped her arms tightly.

"So Sister Andrew has finally managed to persuade you," Sister Rose said. "You'll be studying here for the next four months."

"Three months," Lucy corrected. It seemed an eternity.

"I'll have the heat turned on earlier from now on. We can't have our candidate catching a chill!"

Lucy tried to return Sister Rose's friendly smile, but her mouth refused to move. What would Sister Rose think, and how would she be acting now, if she knew that Lucy had said "Yes" to Sister Andrew without meaning to and without knowing why, that it was only by a kind of silly accident that *she* was here and not Madeleine?

Long after Sister Rose had gone, Lucy stayed next to the radiator, trying to warm herself. She looked up at the strip of dazzling, cloudless, blue sky. It had started already, having to spend time with nuns, having them discussing her among themselves and watching over her, as though she were their child. Sister Andrew had actually called her "my dear child." Lucy shivered again suddenly, remembering what had followed—Sister Andrew's explanation of the study schedule. It was far worse than Lucy had imagined. The regional examinations were scheduled the week before Easter. Until then she'd be working alone in the nuns' study every day after recess, morning and afternoon, then staying after school to review her work with Sister Andrew. She even had to come to school on Saturday mornings.

When Lucy finally turned from the brightness of the window, the room seemed filled with shadow, like a church. She'd never studied alone, in such a quiet place. She'd always done her homework at the kitchen table, and she'd always had to read and study with other people moving around, talking and working noisily. She'd often dreamed of having a place of her very own with a door to close and shut herself away from everything and everyone, a room very much like this one, in fact. But school was the wrong place for it.

As she sat down, Lucy noticed two framed pictures hanging side by side on the opposite wall. Unlike most of the others in Saint Margaret's, these were pictures not of saints but of ordinary farmers in fields that reminded her of places she'd seen just outside Rockford. A metal plate at the bottom of each frame told the name of the artist, Jean Millet, and the picture's title. One was called *The Gleaners* and showed three women bending forward from the waist to pick up something from the ground. Lucy didn't know what *gleaner* meant, but she recognized the title of the other picture, *The Angelus*, as the name of a prayer recited at noon. The man and woman in that picture were standing with their heads bowed, praying.

Their hands looked swollen and sore, and their thick bodies looked tired, as if they were being pressed down into the earth. Just the same, the pictures made the nuns' study seem more like a regular room.

Lucy turned on the table lamp. Its cream-colored shade threw a circle of soft, warm light onto the table and another on the ceiling. She opened one of the books to a page that Sister Andrew had marked with a strip of paper. After she'd read only a few lines the print seemed to melt into an image of her desktop. Its familiar scars and ink stains seemed like old friends compared to this polished table that she'd already marked wherever her hands and fingers had touched it. At this hour the hot, bright sunshine would be flooding in through the classroom window, bringing out the familiar sour smell of the geranium leaves.

She'd never liked her ugly desk, or the pale geranium plants on the windowsill next to it. Now they seemed part of something precious and lost, as though she'd only dreamed them.

5

THE WORK SISTER ANDREW had given her was more
interesting than Lucy had expected, so after a few
days she began to look forward to leaving the
classroom each morning and afternoon after recess to study in the circle of lamplight. It was a
shock afterward to open the door and see the
crowds of students spilling noisily from the coat-
rooms. Although her appearance on the steps to
the nuns' study had caused some people to look
up in curiosity at first, no one noticed her after
the second day. The flow of people moved busily
past her, like water around a rock.

When Lucy went back to the classroom at the end of the afternoon, Laurence was usually there, working glumly at a lesson. One day she offered to help him, meaning only to shorten the wait for Sister Andrew to go over her own work. Laurence accepted, and worked with Lucy so cheerfully that helping him after school became a part of her routine.

"You're good at teaching, Lucy," Laurence remarked one day. "Are you trying for that scholarship so you can be a teacher?"

"No," Lucy answered firmly. "I'll be taking business courses in high school. As soon as I graduate, I'll move to a big city to work in an office. I may even move to another country."

As soon as she saw the excitement in Laurence's eyes, Lucy regretted having told him. She'd never spoken about her plans for the future to anyone at Saint Margaret's except Claire.

Sometimes, while she waited for Laurence to work out a problem, Lucy stood at the classroom window and looked down at the school yard. More and more often she saw Gabriel and his best friend, Raymond, with Madeleine, usually at the center of a group of eighth graders and a few seventh graders who mostly stood by, listening and laughing at Raymond's jokes.

The group was still there late one afternoon by the time Lucy came out of the school. As she approached, she heard Raymond say in a low warning voice, "Watch out! Here comes the brain!"

Lucy joined in the laughter that followed, but she was mortified that Raymond had warned the others, as though he'd seen one of the nuns approaching. On the way home she went over the scene again and again. Raymond might have meant it as a compliment, but even Gabriel had laughed at her being called "the brain," like something out of a horror movie that a mad scientist would keep in a jar.

There was no reason for Raymond or anyone else to call her a brain, because lately the ease she'd always had in doing schoolwork seemed to be slipping away.

"I'm a worse writer now than I was at the beginning," she complained one Saturday afternoon, after Sister Andrew had marked every page of the best essay she'd ever written.

"You're not a worse writer," Sister Andrew said. "You're just breaking old habits. That's always difficult."

In the past Lucy's teachers had always praised her writing. She couldn't see why Sister Andrew's

58

opinion should be so different or why she was trying to make her change, especially after she'd almost forced her to enter the competition.

"What was wrong with my old habits?" Lucy asked.

Any other nun would have been shocked and angry at such a question, but Sister Andrew simply gathered up the scattered, scribbled pages and handed them to Lucy. "The foundation for good writing is there, of course," Sister Andrew said calmly, "but before you can improve, you must rid yourself of the notion that it's easy. It's true that you write well. But you must learn to dig deeper, to examine your ideas. The greatest writers work very hard."

"You mean like Flaubert, the French writer?" Lucy was pleased at the look of surprise on Sister Andrew's face. "I just read a novel that he wrote. It's called *Madame Bovary*."

"Where did you find this book?"

"In the Rockford Public Library. The introduction describes how he sometimes spent days choosing one word."

"From now on I want you to limit the amount of time you spend reading novels. You need to use your spare time for exercise in the fresh air. It will clear your mind, and perhaps you'll struggle less with these." Sister Andrew pointed to the marked-up pages in Lucy's hands. Then she sat back and seemed to relax. "Did you know that *Madame Bovary* was condemned in France when it was first published?"

"Why? I felt sorry for her."

"Then the author has made you feel sorry for a very bad woman."

"But when the priest arrives, she seems to be already dead. That means she can't be forgiven for her sins and won't go to heaven."

These late discussions with Sister Andrew had become Lucy's favorite part of the day. Still, she wished she hadn't said that Madame Bovary wouldn't go to heaven. The priest had arrived too late for Papa, too, and she couldn't believe it had made any difference to God.

Lucy returned *Madame Bovary* to the Rockford Library and didn't stay to wander among the shelves looking for more books to take home. After handing the book to the librarian, she walked out empty-handed.

She started taking the same long walk every Sunday afternoon, passing through the center of town, then through Upper Rockford, which was on higher ground, overlooking the lake. The streets were wider here, and lined on both sides with tall old trees whose branches met at the top in pointed arches, like the ceiling of Saint Margaret's Church. The houses were elegant, like Gabriel's house, and much larger than those on the south side of Rockford, where she lived.

One afternoon just before Christmas she'd gone out of her way to walk through the neighborhood where Gabriel lived, after taking Jeanie downtown to shop for presents. Jeanie had complained about going home by such a roundabout route until the moment she saw the huge Christmas tree in the front window of Gabriel's house. All the lights in the tree were blue, and Lucy and Jeanie had been staring at them in amazement, without speaking, for several minutes when Lucy heard the crunch of footsteps and turned to see Gabriel coming down the walk.

Of course, Jeanie wasn't embarrassed at all at being caught staring at a house by the person who lived there. "Is this your house?" she asked Gabriel.

"Yes," Gabriel answered her with a smile. Then he'd turned to Lucy with a puzzled look.

"We live far from here," Jeanie said, raising her arm and pointing.

Lucy pushed Jeanie's arm down, horrified at the thought of Gabriel standing, as they'd just been doing, and looking at their house. He'd see paint peeling around its doors and windows, and the empty spaces where the bricks had fallen out again after Papa had repaired them. Worse than any of that was the ugly square turret jutting out to one side of their house that made it seem ready to tip over. The turret contained the stairway landings and looked added on, as though the builders had forgotten to make room for them. The landing windows had no curtains, so from the outside they seemed to be staring blankly at the sky, like the windows of an empty, haunted house.

"We don't have our Christmas tree yet," Jeanie was telling Gabriel cheerfully. "We have a cousin who sells them. He's letting us pick one from the ones left over on Christmas Eve."

Lucy couldn't think of a way to stop Jeanie's chatter without seeming bossy. When she glanced at Gabriel, she saw that he was watching Jeanie's face as if he didn't want to miss a word of what she was saying. "*We* have lights in *all* the colors," Jeanie said proudly, encouraged by Gabriel's friendly, close attention. Then she turned and looked again at his house. "But blue lights are very pretty too," she said politely, as though she didn't really think so.

Lucy couldn't remember walking home afterward, except that she'd listened numbly to Jeanie describing her plans to wrap the presents she'd just bought.

At the time of their meeting in front of his house, Lucy's climbs and talks with Gabriel after school had already ended. She'd never found out what he had thought on finding her standing there with her little sister on a cold, dark afternoon, so far out of the way to their own house.

Past the northern edge of town the land was covered with forest. In spite of the hard climb, this was Lucy's favorite place to walk. Only quiet sounds, such as a clump of snow falling from a pine tree or the song of a wintering bird, broke the stillness.

A walk to the south of town would have been dangerous, so Lucy never went there. The barren, rocky land that she could see from the window of the attic landing appeared to be flat, but in fact rose gradually and steadily until it reached the edge of Lake Griffith. There it dropped off suddenly in a high, curved wall of sheer rock that fell straight down, far beneath the surface of the lake. The water here was so deep that, as far as Lucy knew, it had never been measured.

On bright days the blinding glare of sunlight on snow made it easy to miss the edge and fall to the frozen lake hundreds of feet below. And on cloudy days the dull light flattened everything, so the lake's snow-covered surface looked as if it were on the same level as the land instead of far down. Like all the children in Rockford, Lucy had been warned to stay far away from the cliff.

One day, instead of walking through the woods, Lucy wandered through new curving streets beyond the edge of town where houses were being built. The front door of one house had blown open. She went inside and walked slowly through all the rooms, breathing in the smell of new wood and looking out every window. She stayed, examining everything including the pipes and wiring in the unfinished walls, until it was too dark to see. On her way out she swept away the snow that had drifted inside the entryway and pushed in the button on the new doorknob so that the door would lock behind her.

In the weeks that followed, while she was working in the nuns' study, Lucy closed her eyes and imagined the work that was probably being done on the house at that moment. She went by it every Sunday from then on, but she never again found the door unlocked. She didn't mind, because it meant that the house was safe. Besides, she was sure that one day she'd live in a house just like that, with nothing in it that was faded or rusted or broken. Her house would have no dark corners, no freezing attic, no turret, nothing ugly or haunted-looking. Her house would be filled with light, and everything in it would be fresh and new.

6

NOW THAT SHE HAD to go to school on Saturday mornings, Lucy was getting up extra early to finish her weekly chores. Otherwise she'd have to do them in the afternoon, and every Saturday afternoon most of the people she knew at Saint Margaret's, including Gabriel, went to the Arcadian Theatre to see whatever movie was playing that week.

The Arc was unlike any place Lucy had ever been in. It had a very high ceiling with a dome at the center. The ceiling was dark blue and sprinkled with silver stars. But the dome was gold and glowed richly above tiny lights set close together in a circle around its base, like a halo. The side walls were painted with scenes of ancient castles, gardens, arched walkways, and arbors draped in dense green vines. The carpeting was red with a pattern of exotic flowers and leaves. Its thickness muffled all sounds, so when the movie was about to start and the lights dimmed, the darkness felt velvety and cushioned. Once, while she and Jeanie had been waiting for the movie to begin, Jeanie had looked up at the ceiling and asked Lucy, "Do you suppose the houses in heaven are like this?" Although she laughed, Lucy remembered asking Victor almost the same question. She still couldn't imagine a more peaceful, beautiful place to be than inside the Arc.

One of Lucy's weekly chores was to clean the bathroom. On a Saturday morning in early February she paused on her way up the stairs with her mop and pail and stood for a moment in the bright winter sunshine streaming in through the landing window. She'd met Edward coming up from the cellar a few minutes earlier and offered to trade jobs with him. Although he was bundled against the cold and carrying the snow shovel to clear the porches and sidewalk of a heavy snowfall the night before, Edward had refused.

In the bathroom Lucy set down the mop and pail and pushed the window up as high as it would go. She leaned far out and looked around. Every housetop, bush, even the smallest tree branch, was covered with a layer of new snow.

Lucy had been taking deep breaths of the clean, crisp air for several minutes before she realized that Edward was standing directly below her. If he had moved or made the slightest sound, she would have noticed him right away. But Edward was standing perfectly still with both hands on the handle of the upright shovel, his face turned to one side toward the back of the house. He seemed to be watching or listening to something, but Lucy saw nothing that would draw such complete attention from Edward. The only sound she heard was the soft crunch of tires rolling over the new snow when a car passed by in the street.

She cupped her hands around her mouth and was about to yell down and scare Edward out of his daydream when she heard another, even quieter sound—the scraping and slicing of ice skates. By pushing her shoulders out even farther, Lucy was able to see a part of the ice rink in Alice's backyard. The rink had been cleared of snow, and Alice was practicing her school figures, moving in and out of Lucy's line of vision. She disappeared, then reappeared, following the same pattern over and over. Because she was looking down to watch the traces her skate blades had made in the ice, Alice seemed not to have noticed Edward watching her in a kind of trance.

Alice was wearing her outdoor practice outfit, a white angora sweater and a short, dark-gray circle skirt with matching wool tights. Mama had sewn the skirt and the round gray cap that was perched on the back of Alice's head. Alice's blond hair curled out from the edge of her cap, and when she skated forward the curls blew gently back from her face. When she turned her head to look back, her hair was pushed forward against her cheeks.

Although she sewed Alice's skating outfits exactly the way Alice and her mother asked, Mama didn't approve of them. "A skirt like this hardly covers anything," she'd say to Lucy, "so what's the use of it?"

Lucy had never told Mama how much she wanted a short circle skirt just like the one Alice had on today, but she hoped to talk Mama into making one for her just as soon as she could skate well enough to wear it without looking silly.

But even Mama would have agreed that Alice looked especially nice this morning. With her head bent in perfect concentration and the sun shining all around her, Alice looked like a picture

Lucy had once seen of an angel at prayer in a shower of golden light.

Edward had no right to be watching in that sneaky way, especially after what he'd said to Alice only yesterday. Alice had come over to show Lucy her new short haircut and curly permanent. "It's called 'The Friz,' " Alice had explained with a laugh.

"Weren't you afraid your tiny brain would frizzle up too?" Edward asked her.

He deserved to be caught spying on Alice. On Lucy's left, almost within reach of the bathroom window, hung the giant icicle that formed there every year from melted snow that collected and ran down an inside corner of the roof. This year the icicle had grown to more than a foot thick and over five feet long. A slight tap was all it would take to break off the tip, which would then fall right next to Edward. With luck, it might even land right on his head. Laughing soundlessly at the thought of Edward suddenly jumping aside with a yell that would let Alice know he was there, Lucy carefully eased the floor mop through the open window. She gave the icicle a slight tap with the end of the mop handle, then brought it quickly back inside.

Several seconds passed, but nothing seemed to

be happening. Lucy leaned out, gave the icicle a much harder tap with the mop handle, and immediately heard a long, slow cracking from far above. The icicle was breaking away from the roof, all in one piece. Lucy looked down and saw the long, sharp tip trembling, and below it Edward standing exactly as before, and only a few inches to one side of the massive icicle. If she shouted to warn him, he might move the wrong way and be standing right under it when it fell.

Lucy was still trying to figure out what to do when she heard a loud snap, then felt a rush of cold air. Her eyes blinked shut with terror as the icicle dropped past her. They opened just in time to see the icicle crash onto the frozen ground, only slightly to one side of Edward's feet. Fragments of ice slashed through the new-fallen snow in every direction. Seen from above, their tracks formed a giant star, exactly like a cartoon drawing of an explosion.

Edward stood perfectly still for several seconds before leaping away from the wall. He looked up and saw Lucy. "Are you completely crazy?" he screamed.

Lucy still hadn't moved. Her hands were holding the mop outside the window as she stared back down at Edward. Except for the round patches of red on his cheeks, Edward's angry, upturned face was almost as dead-white as the snow.

"Just a couple of inches closer!" Edward screamed, then tore off his mitten with his teeth and spat it onto the ground. "This much closer," he held two fingers out, slightly apart, "and a ton of ice would've come down right on top of me! I could have been killed!" On the last word, *killed*, Edward's voice cracked. He'd started to cry, even though Alice was now watching from the near end of the rink.

Lucy slowly pulled the mop inside, then put her head out again. "It wasn't a ton of ice," she told Edward. "Anyway, I was sure you wouldn't move. In fact, you looked as if you might freeze to death from standing there so long, staring at Alice."

Edward shook his bare fist at Lucy, then picked up the snow shovel. He held it for a moment, as if trying to remember what it was, then threw it down again and stomped out of sight past the corner of the house. He was heading straight for the back door, Lucy knew. "There's a dangerous lunatic upstairs," he'd tell Mama. "She should be locked up before she hurts somebody."

Lucy was still at the window, shocked at what she'd done. "Lucy!" Alice called to her. "You could have some good skating practice this afternoon. Our whole family will be out."

Alice spoke as if nothing unusual had happened. But Lucy couldn't think of anything besides the fact that what Edward had said was true. What she had thought would be only a harmless prank had almost killed her brother.

While she waited for Lucy to answer, Alice moved her feet in tiny curves and circles, like a butterfly or a bird that couldn't keep still. She didn't seem to mind that Edward had been watching her. She might even have known all along, Lucy realized.

"My dad flooded this two nights ago," Alice said, "and the ice is still perfect except for one crack, right here, that you should watch for." She drew the blade of her skate along a mark in the ice.

"Thanks," Lucy called back, "but I probably won't have time to practice today."

She pulled her head inside, closed the window, and rolled down the green window shade. The dim green sunlight filtering through was like being caught underwater. Lucy had to sit down on the edge of the tub. She'd refused Alice's invitation without telling her the reason. But she didn't want to remind Alice that she had to go to school on Saturdays. And she didn't want to remind herself that what she had to practice there was drab and hidden, without beauty or magic, nothing that could compare with what Alice had been doing, which was so graceful and pretty that it had completely hypnotized Edward.

Lucy was late arriving at school that morning and worked longer with Sister Andrew to make up the time. Afterward she ran all the way to the Arc but found the doors already closed. The woman in the glass ticket booth was counting tickets and money. She didn't look up when Lucy approached to ask how long ago the movie had started. Lucy looked at the pictures outside the entrance. They were all of soldiers running through clouds of smoke carrying rifles or lying crumpled on gray, torn-up earth. She wouldn't have been able to watch a war movie anyway, now that she knew the soldiers were people like Victor, with fathers and mothers and sisters, and that they really died.

Lucy didn't feel like going home. While she stood there wondering what to do, the theater's electric sign flickered above her head, then flashed on. The sign was arc shaped, like a rainbow, and painted with stripes in rainbow colors. Along each stripe a row of round light bulbs turned on and off in sequence, so that the light seemed to be moving downward as if spilling into a painted black pot with yellow neon circles inside it representing gold coins.

The day had turned cloudy by the time she'd come out of Saint Margaret's School, and the bright, moving lights of the Arcadian Theatre sign made the sky seem even more somber and dull. A long time ago Victor had brought her downtown after dark to show her these lights. She must have been very little then, because she remembered being held up in Victor's arms and hearing him laugh when she reached out and tried to catch one of the lights. She thought they were falling toward her.

Jeanie was in the kitchen playing with the twins when Lucy got home. "Tessa got a job today washing people's hair at the beauty parlor," Jeanie explained. "She's paying me to help Mama take care of Paul-ette. Want to play with us for a while? We're playing school. You can be the teacher."

Lucy shook her head and went straight through the front hall. The sound of Mama's sewing machine coming from the living room reminded her of what had happened that morning with the icicle. If Mama found out that she was home, she'd call her in to talk about it. Lucy took her skates from the hall closet and slipped out the front door.

Alice's rink seemed drab and abandoned without the sunshine, and especially without Alice to skate with. After putting her skates on, Lucy circled the rink several times as fast as she could to get warm, then slowed down and continued circling mechanically.

After a while the ache in her legs and ankles melted away. The air was very still and warm. Although a few large snowflakes were floating down through the gathering dark, Lucy took off her coat and threw it on a low bank of snow at the far end of the rink. She hadn't stopped to change out of the convent tunic she'd worn to school that morning. Without a coat the loose tunic felt light and allowed her to move so freely that she was able to imagine herself in a proper skating outfit.

Lucy made a neat turn and skated smoothly backward. She was keeping her knees slightly bent, and her body was perfectly relaxed. As she picked up speed, her arms rose naturally for balance. She turned forward, then backward again with the quick movement that always came so easily to Alice but that she'd never even come close to before.

All around, in one window after another, lights

were being turned on. Other people were very close by, yet she was alone in a silence so complete that she could hear her own breathing and the whisper of her clothes as she moved. It was snowing steadily now, and the ice was covered with a thin layer of snow, so she could see the clear marks of her skates.

She traced two large circles in the form of a figure eight, then retraced them several times. She tried a low jump, landed perfectly on her right foot, and glided smoothly backward. She jumped again. This jump was higher and longer, but when she landed her ankle wobbled and she fell over onto one hand. She brushed the snow from her glove, then tried again, faster, turned neatly in midair, and made a solid landing.

Lucy had no idea what time it was. It was dark now, except for the light from the surrounding windows that made the snowy air glow faintly. She wished that Gabriel could see her moving so easily and smoothly. She tried to imagine how she must look, a shadow turning and gliding through the semidark. Suddenly the ice seemed to rise up and become a wall that she slammed into hard, with the full length of her body. A burning pain flashed through her stomach, her chest, and one side of her face. The lighted windows, the curtain of falling snow, the snowbank, were at a peculiar angle, as if the world had tipped over on its side. Then she realized that she was lying flat against the ice.

She couldn't breathe. The inside of her chest felt flat and dry, like an envelope, with no space at all for air. She opened her mouth and tried frantically to call out. No sound came. She was about to die here on Alice's rink, unable to call for help, surrounded by houses filled with people who would rush out if only they knew what was happening. Her own mother was probably in the kitchen fixing supper, only a few feet away.

At the thought of Mama, a faint moan passed through Lucy's throat. A thread of air slid into her lungs. It hurt, yet she was so happy to be breathing that she laughed. Laughing pulled more air in, so she was able to push herself up to a sitting position. She was shivering hard from lying on the ice without a coat, but her throat and lungs, and one side of her face where it had struck the ice, all felt as if they were on fire.

She realized now what had happened. Her skate had caught in the crack that Alice had warned her about. The falling snow had gradually filled it in, then covered it so that she'd forgotten completely that it was there. Her fall had been sudden, and to anyone watching she must have looked exactly like a clown pretending to slip on a banana peel. Lucy laughed again, and more air flowed in, cooling her burning lungs. In spite of the cold she wanted only to sit on the ice and go on breathing. The burning on her face had become a pleasing warmth, and each breath filled her with joy.

One of her gloves had come off when she fell. It was lying on the ice a few feet away, its fingers round and curled inward gently at the tips, like a hand letting the snowflakes gather peacefully in its palm. Lucy gazed at it with amazement. Snow was falling everywhere, on the houses and fences, on the snowbank next to Alice's rink, on Tessa's old convent tunic, covering everything as if it wanted to protect each thing equally.

7

LUCY WAS LYING on her side on Alice's white satin bedspread after wiping the stage makeup from her face. It was almost time to go home. Alice sat at her dressing table, leaning close to the mirror to examine the blue eye shadow she'd just brushed on.

"I'll have to try this in rehearsal to see if it runs when I sweat," she said with a sigh. "I always have to rehearse for the Ice Carnival later than anybody else because I'm doing a special solo and it has to be perfect." She turned around and looked at Lucy. "It's supposed to be a big surprise, so I have to stay and practice after everybody's gone. It was my mother's idea, and my coach says nothing like it has ever been seen in Rockford before. I'm afraid the audience will hate it and there I'll be, out on the ice all by myself, feeling stupid."

Lucy turned carefully onto her back and stared up at the frilled canopy over Alice's bed. Her ribs were still sore from her fall on the ice, but she hadn't told Alice or anyone else about it.

"I thought you *liked* skating in front of people," she said. "You're so good at it. Everybody thinks so."

"Everybody thinks *you're* smart, Lucy, but you don't seem to like that very much," Alice said.

"I'd much rather be good at dancing and skating."

Alice laughed. "I'd much rather be good at getting to know some of the boys at school. Wouldn't you?"

"Only one boy," Lucy murmured. She rolled to the edge of the bed and let herself slide off slowly and comically. When she touched the floor, she groaned and wrapped her arms around her ribs.

"What's the matter?" Alice asked.

"I fell while I was practicing jumps on your rink the other day," Lucy confessed.

"You mean the day you made the icicle fall on Edward?"

"It didn't fall *on* him!"

So much had gone wrong all the same, in the last few days, as if to pay her back for what she'd done. For one thing, the weather that had turned suddenly warm that afternoon had started thawing Alice's rink almost from the moment Lucy had started to skate the way she'd always dreamed of. The next day Mrs. Palmer had asked Lucy to help Alice with this week's French homework. "She's fallen behind since you started studying for that scholarship," Mrs. Palmer said, "and since Alice will be too busy rehearsing for the Ice Carnival to give you skating lessons, I'll pay you for your help." They'd always worked in Alice's room with books and papers spread out on the floor or on the bed. Every few minutes the lessons had come to a stop because they'd had to hunt for a pencil that had disappeared among the folds of Alice's satin bedspread or because something in the lesson had struck them as funny.

This time, because Lucy was being paid, they'd had to work at the dining-room table with Mrs. Palmer sitting across from them, knitting and listening. In the past the lessons in Alice's high school French text had been easy, but now Lucy hadn't recognized some of the words. She hadn't known what a *croissant* was even though it turned out to be a common type of bread that everyone in France ate for breakfast. And she'd never heard of *café au lait*, either, but according to Alice's book it was the other thing that everybody in France had for breakfast.

When this happened, Alice gave Lucy a friendly, teasing poke with her foot under the table, but Mrs. Palmer looked up sharply. Lucy was ashamed not to know words that even beginners like Alice were learning. "Everybody I know eats toast in the morning and drinks cocoa or tea," she told Mrs. Palmer.

"Tea is more of an English drink," Mrs. Palmer said. "I don't suppose they drink it in France. I hope you're teaching Alice proper French and not the French-Canadian kind."

After the lesson Alice had invited Lucy to stay and listen to some special music on the Palmers' new record player. It was called *The Afternoon of a Faun*. "It's by Claude Debussy. He's French," Alice explained as she slid the record carefully from its cover. "I'd like to skate to it sometime, but with a partner, maybe someone who looks like this." Alice laughed, and handed the cover to Lucy. On it was a picture of a young man wearing what looked like an animal's skin. He was sitting on a rock surrounded by a misty forest and holding a reed flute up to his mouth. His hair, though it was blond, was tightly curled, and reminded Lucy of Gabriel's hair, except for the two small horns just above the forehead.

Alice played the record several times, and they listened with their eyes closed, their heads propped on cushions as they lay on the Palmers' thick, soft living-room carpet. It was the most beautiful music Lucy had ever heard, with notes so delicate and held for so long that they seemed to lift and carry her, like the floating that happened only in dreams. She imagined herself skating like Alice, with Gabriel as her partner. She could almost feel their smooth, perfectly matched movements as they flowed together over the ice in perfect time with the music.

When she was on her way home from Alice's that night, a car passed by Lucy, then stopped just ahead of her. When she caught up with it, the car started again and followed her slowly around the corner. She walked faster until she was running, too frightened to turn around and see if the car was still there.

Once she was inside the front hall, the sight of her bed made Lucy feel even worse. The floor all around it was littered with threads and scraps of cloth that had been dragged in as people passed through from the living room, where Mama was sewing. Lucy had a dry, sick taste in her mouth from running and being so afraid, but she couldn't go in and tell Mama what had happened. Mama would be so worried that she'd make her come home from Alice's before dark from now on.

Lucy lay awake for a long time. She tried to erase the image of the car following her by listening to the music again in her mind, but she could remember only a few disconnected fragments, which played over and over in her head until her body was stiff from the effort to remember more. When she moved to find a more comfortable position, the bed rocked from side to side like a creaking, unsteady ship.

The thaw continued. The weather became so warm that even though it was still early February, Lucy walked to school one day without a hat or gloves, and with her coat unbuttoned. The sky was covered with low clouds, and the edges of buildings were dripping with melted snow that fell in gentle, steady drops, like the sound of spring rain. A soft wind blew, carrying threads of a spicy, smoky perfume that seemed to Lucy to be coming from far-off countries. It made her want more than ever to get away from Rockford, away from Saint Margaret's. But it was also a sign that spring was approaching and, more important, so was the end of her studies for the competition.

She was wearing a scarf that Tessa had brought home. Someone had left it in the beauty shop and never come back for it even though it was pure silk with rose-, plum-, and wine-colored Oriental flowers. When the wind lifted the ends of the scarf, the silk felt smooth against her face.

She was feeling light and happy for the first time in weeks, as if approaching the end of a long, dark tunnel. The warm, springlike day seemed so filled with hope that when Lucy heard running footsteps behind her, she didn't turn around, thinking it might be Gabriel. She'd had very few chances to speak with him, and each time there'd been other people present. She'd been afraid of saying or doing something that would show how she felt. She could almost hear the gossip: "Did you know the brain is madly in love with Gabriel Sinclair?"

It was Claire. "I called and called you," Claire said, laughing and out of breath, "but you went right on without hearing me." She took Lucy's arm. "What were you thinking about? Or was it a *who?*"

Alarmed at having her thoughts read, even by Claire, Lucy ignored the joke and said seriously as they walked on together, "I was afraid you weren't ever coming back to school. I've asked Sister Andrew to let me take your work to your house, but she told me it wasn't necessary."

"She's been sending it with my little brother, but I don't have time to do it. I'm not coming back today either, and I won't be for a while."

"It's awful at school without you," Lucy said fervently. "You've been absent such a long time, and I've hardly seen you since before Christmas."

"My mother had complications after the baby was born, and she's still very weak. I'm on my way to the drugstore now to have a prescription filled, and I thought I'd walk with you part of the way." They walked in silence; then Claire said quietly, "Thank you for bringing those things your mother sent for the baby. I'm sorry I couldn't invite you to stay. If we had a telephone, at least I could call you once in a while!" Claire laughed. "Things are in even more of a mess than usual. But my mother *is* getting better." Suddenly Claire let go of Lucy's arm and stood back. "What do you think of my new coat?"

Instead of the usual lumpy clothes that were either too big or too small, Claire was wearing a coat that fit perfectly. It looked almost new, with a wide, stiff collar that she'd turned up in back. The collar hid most of Claire's rough, stubbly haircut, which no longer looked too short, but stylish and almost pretty. Claire's face looked different too. Although her skin was pink and raw-looking, it was smooth and clear.

Claire was smiling proudly, but with her mouth closed, as usual, to hide her teeth.

"You look awfully nice," Lucy said.

Claire had moved close again and tucked her hand under Lucy's arm. "My dad got a job cleaning the new doctors' building downtown," she explained. "One of them's a skin doctor, and he's giving me treatments for free. Later on the dentist will fix my teeth. It's part of my dad's wages. The skin doctor's name is Dr. Steven Precious, and he's every bit as handsome and nice as his name! I have to wash my face three times a day with soap that smells just like tar." Claire brushed her cheek with her fingers, then stopped and pulled her hand away. "I almost forgot! You're not supposed to touch your face, except to wash it. Dr. Precious says that makeup and creams are bad for the skin. Did you know that?"

"No," Lucy said, uneasy that Claire seemed so changed. "What about the cream they use in hospitals? That can't be bad for the skin, or nurses wouldn't use it on patients, right?"

"Who told you that?"

"Sister Rose."

Claire laughed. "You mean you've been having conversations with Old Lima Bean?"

"Sister Rose," Lucy said, deliberately using the correct name, "is much nicer than people think, once you get to know her."

"I was just making fun of her, like we always did." After a silence Claire said softly, "I miss school so much. I miss you, Lucy. I even miss Old Lima Bean—I mean *Sister Rose*," she teased, squeezing Lucy's arm.

Lucy laughed. "I miss you too," she said. "When *are* you coming back? You'll have to sometime, won't you?"

"I don't know. The truant officer came to our house. He took one look around and left. My mother almost lost the baby when it was born. There was so much bleeding, the doctor didn't even want to move her to the hospital. My dad had been drinking, and we couldn't wake him up enough to help, so I had to."

"What did you do?"

"I had to look for something to raise the foot of the bed," Claire said in the flat tone of voice that Lucy recognized as the signal that Claire didn't want to talk anymore about something that had happened at home.

"I wish *I* had a coat like that," Lucy said, to change the subject. "You still haven't told me where it came from."

Claire's face brightened. "Mrs. Precious, the doctor's wife, gave it to me. It's called 'coachman style' because of the collar." Claire picked up the corners of the wide collar and held them together in front of her face so that only her eyes were visible. "Mrs. Precious and I are exactly the same size," Claire said from behind the collar. "We even wear the same size shoes!" Her eyes sparkled mischievously at Lucy.

"I should turn here," Claire said when they reached a corner. "But I'll walk with you the rest of the way. I want to hear all about your good news, Lucy."

Lucy stopped in surprise. "What good news?"

"I mean the scholarship, silly!"

"Oh that. How did you find out? Hardly anybody knows."

Claire laughed. "*Everybody* knows, Lucy. Besides, Sister Andrew told me last September that she was going to ask you to represent Saint Margaret's."

"She told *you* first?" Lucy walked on angrily. "And you didn't say a word to me?"

"She made me promise not to, so I never did,

even though I wanted so much to let you know. I thought you'd be pleased."

"What did she say? Why were the two of you talking about me behind my back in the first place?"

"I asked her if she knew of any scholarships I might try for. I thought that since she'd been to so many places before coming to Saint Margaret's, she might know of a way for me to get into a convent school."

"Aren't you coming to Rockford High? Why do you want to go to a convent school?"

Claire hesitated, then said quietly, "Because I think I want to become a nun."

"Like Old Lima Bean?" Lucy asked, watching Claire's eyes for the glint of light that would show she'd been joking.

But it didn't appear. "No, not like that. The kind of nun who stays inside the convent." Claire let out a deep sigh and tilted her head back to push the high collar down.

"What did Sister Andrew say when you told her? Did she tell you what a lucky girl you were to have a religious vocation?"

"No, she hardly said anything. She said I had a fine mind."

"I don't call that hardly saying anything. She's

never told *me* I had a fine mind. In fact, she told me I shouldn't fish for compliments."

"She did say something about a vocation. She said even if I have one, it might be best to attend a public high school for a while. Don't you think that's a strange thing for a nun to say?"

They'd arrived at Saint Margaret's School and stood in silence at the edge of the school yard. Noisy games were in progress everywhere, and coats lay scattered on the gray, wet snow.

"*You* should be competing for that scholarship, not me," Lucy said. "I didn't want to. I still don't."

"Sister Andrew said she had to be realistic. School had just started and I'd already been absent. I knew I wouldn't have enough time to study. She said she'd help me find another way and that you had the best chance. I thought so too. I may not even finish the eighth grade this year."

Lucy's throat tightened. "I could have helped you. I could help you now."

"We both have too much to do," Claire said. "I'm glad Sister Andrew chose you and not Madeleine. Can you imagine what that would be like?" Claire lifted her chin very high and looked down her nose at Lucy.

Lucy laughed. "When you're a nun, you won't be allowed to make fun of other people like that!"

Claire's expression turned serious. "I know," she said quietly. "I'll have to give up a lot of things. I'll probably never go out with a boy, for instance. You'll have to tell me what it's like."

"I'll probably never know what it's like to go out with a boy," Lucy said. "You'll have to ask Madeleine. She and Raymond and Gabriel Sinclair are always together now. If a boy ever pays *any* attention to me, it will be a miracle."

"You mean they'll build a church on the spot where it happens?" Claire teased. Lucy couldn't help smiling. "That's not what I meant, though," Claire said. "What's it like, preparing for those exams?" she asked seriously.

"There's nothing to tell," Lucy said impatiently. "All I do is read, write, and memorize whatever I'm told to read, write, and memorize. I'm just waiting for it to be over."

Claire studied Lucy's face for a long moment. "I only wanted to know so I could picture you working and studying," she said softly. "You're going to be late," she added, pointing at the school yard. The class lines had formed and were already filing into the school.

"I'm often late these days," Lucy said. "Nobody says anything, not even Sister Rose." When the front door had closed on the last line, Lucy saw that Claire's eyes were shiny with tears. "Sister

Andrew should have let you try for that scholarship," she said gently. "It isn't fair!"

Claire shrugged. "No. My dad's friends come over and play cards until around midnight, when he leaves for work. I'd be much too tired all the time to study, even without the new baby and missing so much school. In a convent everything would be clean and quiet, and I could be by myself once in a while."

"Then you *ought* to be the one studying for the competition," Lucy said, laughing. "The nuns' study has all the quiet and being alone anybody could want!" But Claire didn't laugh.

Lucy suddenly took off the silk scarf and draped it around Claire's neck. "I want you to have this," she said, "in case you *do* decide to give up everything and become a nun." Claire lifted the scarf and held it against her face.

"But do you really want to take vows and be shut up inside a convent for the rest of your life?" Lucy asked.

"Maybe not. It just seems to me that it must be a kind of heaven, with regular times for work and meals and sleep. In a convent you always know what you'll be doing next, even if it's only housecleaning. I mean conventcleaning." Claire looked up with a sudden smile that made her eyes shine.

Lucy reached over and knotted the scarf. "I'll

tell you anything you want to know about what I'm doing for the exams," she promised.

"Thank you," Claire said when Lucy had finished draping the scarf carefully over the wide collar of her new coat. She stood perfectly still, like a child being dressed, then turned quickly and set off in the direction from which they'd come.

8

ONE DAY SISTER ANDREW gave Lucy a long poem to memorize. "Mother Augusta has agreed to prepare you for the elocution part of the competition. From now on you will practice with her twice a week at noon in the convent music room."

When Lucy walked up to the convent the next day, all its white window curtains were closed as usual. Unlike most students at Saint Margaret's, she'd seldom thought about what the covered windows might be concealing, but now that she was about to go inside it, the convent seemed more secretive and forbidding than ever.

She pressed the doorbell and heard its faint ring, followed by such a long, deep silence that she began to hope no one would answer. The door was opened suddenly by a nun who seemed not much older than Lucy. She wore a long, dark-blue apron, and the sleeves of her black habit had been rolled back above her elbows. Her hands were wrinkled and red, as if they'd been in hot water for a long time.

The young nun did not speak and kept her eyes lowered as she stepped back to let Lucy into a small, square entryway; then she opened another door and disappeared inside the convent. Lucy stood alone in a dim, closetlike entry with dark wooden doors on three sides. The little nun had pointed to one door, but Lucy couldn't tell if she was supposed to open it and go in, or wait.

Lucy decided to wait. She dreaded meeting Mother Augusta, who was very tall and imposing, especially when she sat at the church organ high above the choir. Once, during a service, Claire had signaled to Lucy to look up at Mother Augusta, whose arms were stretched wide to reach both the ends of the keyboard at the same time. "What does that remind you of?" Claire had whispered.

"A giant bat." Lucy had understood Claire perfectly. They'd had to sit without looking at each other throughout the rest of the service to keep from laughing.

A sudden burst of piano music from beyond the music-room door caused Lucy to jump in fright. But the clear, perfect notes continued, racing up and down, then up again, until the cramped entry seemed filled with delicate, crystal steps of sound.

The music stopped as abruptly as it had begun. Lucy heard voices, and a moment later the door to the music room opened. Madeleine came out carrying a leather music case. She closed the door behind her, then leaned on it and began to fasten the straps of her music case. When Lucy reached forward and held the case to steady it, Madeleine said, "Thanks," without looking up.

Lucy watched Madeleine's fingers struggle to push the straps through the narrow buckles. She found it hard to believe that such ordinary, fumbling fingers had produced the rapid, magical sounds she'd just heard. "I didn't know you could play the piano so well," she said.

"Thank you." Madeleine was pulling on her gloves. "Mother Augusta wants you to wait until she calls you." She smiled at Lucy with friendly interest. "Are you taking piano lessons now?"

"No." Lucy laughed shyly. Ever since she could remember, Papa had said that his "favorite wish" would be to have all his children take music lessons. "We don't even have a piano."

"You don't need a piano," Madeleine said. "Mother Augusta lets her students practice here." She pointed back over her shoulder.

Madeleine's casual gesture toward the closed door caused Lucy's nervousness to come rushing back. She was afraid Madeleine might ask why she was waiting to see Mother Augusta, if not for a music lesson. "What was that piece you were playing, the fast one at the end?"

"That wasn't a piece." Madeleine laughed and opened the front door. "It was only a finger exercise."

Embarrassed at her mistake, Lucy asked quickly, "Do you ever play *Afternoon of a Faun* by Claude Debussy?"

Madeleine brushed back her long hair with one hand. "I know that composer, but not that title," she said, frowning slightly. "Are you sure it's correct?"

"Yes. I've heard it several times on a record— played on a flute, though, not a piano."

"Lucy Delaroche! Please come in now." Mother Augusta's deep voice interrupted from inside the music room.

Lucy was pleased at the look of friendly sympathy on Madeleine's face, as though she and Lucy were suddenly alike. "I'll ask about that piece if you like," Madeleine said.

"Thanks," Lucy said. "It's my favorite."

The music room was long and narrow, with windows along one side, so as she stood there Lucy could be seen by anyone passing by on the street. Mother Augusta was at the far end sitting on the piano bench with her back to the piano. She motioned to Lucy to approach, then leaned back with her elbows on the closed keyboard cover. The black skirt of her nun's habit was spread out on both sides, almost covering the wide bench.

Lucy was glad she'd memorized the poem perfectly the night before. It was very long and told the story of a man who decided to cross a frozen river with his wife and children in a heavy, horse-drawn sleigh in spite of warnings that the ice was breaking up. When the sleigh, with the family on it, was still only halfway across, darkness fell and they lost their way. The ice, which was thinner at the center of the river, began to crack under the weight of the sleigh. The man whipped his terrified horses to make them pull harder, but as they struggled, their hooves only broke faster through the ice, dragging the sleigh down into the water. The children screamed and the parents prayed, but the dark, freezing-cold water continued to rise around them until it closed over their heads.

The poem ended with a description of the sounds of water quietly lapping and pieces of ice gently tapping against each other, and of the moon coming out from behind a thick bank of clouds to shine down on the dark, jagged hole in the ice.

Mother Augusta listened closely while Lucy recited the entire poem in a high-pitched, trembling voice. "At the end I want you to do this," Mother Augusta said, raising her right hand to one side above her head, then bringing it smoothly at an angle across her body until it was pointing at the floor. Lucy understood that the movement was supposed to represent rays of moonlight shining down, but when she tried it, her hand came down stiffly and much too fast.

"It might help if you thought of me as your panel of judges," Mother Augusta said. "You don't want to give them the impression of someone chopping wood, do you?"

Lucy was stung by the mention of judges. Sister Andrew had never mentioned judges, and until this moment Lucy hadn't ever thought about the strangers who would read what she wrote on the exams and who would be watching and listening while she recited this long, depressing poem.

From that day on Lucy couldn't stop thinking about the judges. She felt their presence everywhere, reading her work over her shoulder and shaking their heads disapprovingly at her recitation, which only became clumsier each time she practiced it in front of Sister Augusta.

One day when Lucy was crossing the school yard, she heard someone call her name. She turned and saw Madeleine, walking between Raymond and Gabriel, waving to her to come over. "I asked Mother Augusta today about that music you were talking about," she said as Lucy approached.

"Thank you," Lucy said, flattered that Madeleine had remembered their conversation. Gabriel, she noticed, had turned their way and was listening.

But when Lucy reached her side, Madeleine continued, "Mother Augusta told me to tell you that she never uses that sort of music for her lessons, because it's pagan and improper, and that you shouldn't even be listening to it."

Lucy backed away, her face burning. Gabriel was looking at her with surprise, but she couldn't tell if he was shocked at the humiliating message that Madeleine had repeated in front of everybody, or at Lucy for asking about music that Mother Augusta said was improper.

Lucy couldn't eat her lunch that day, and finally had to stop eating any of the lunches Mama prepared for her to take to school on the days she had recitation practice. If she ate before she had to stand in front of Mother Augusta, the food stayed in a tight, dry lump in her chest and made breathing almost impossible while she was reciting. After practice she was too exhausted to be hungry. So that Mama wouldn't know that she hadn't eaten, she started giving her lunches to Laurence when she helped him after class.

Lucy found a way to avoid meeting anyone by walking at the far edge of the school yard. But on the day before Valentine's Day she heard her name called again. This time it was Raymond. Lucy glanced back, then walked on. "Hey Lucy, wait a minute!" he yelled, louder this time. When she heard him running toward her, Lucy turned around and saw that Madeleine and some of the others were following close behind. Gabriel wasn't among them, and they were all looking at her with expectant smiles on their faces.

"Somebody asked me to give you this!" Raymond held out a tiny box covered in blue velvet. It was so pretty that without thinking, Lucy reached forward and took it. It was the kind of box that came from a jewelry store, with rounded corners and a hinged top. Lucy held it on her open palm and wondered what to do. The crowd was now all around her, and people had started whispering and laughing among themselves without taking their eyes off her.

It had to be one of Raymond's jokes, Lucy decided, although it looked like a gift. The others had come to watch her open it. Something unpleasant or frightening would happen when she did. "Thank you," she said, smiling at Raymond exactly as though she really had received a gift from him. Then she pushed the box inside her coat pocket and hurried on, half running, toward the convent.

Raymond followed along beside her. "Why don't you open it, Lucy?" he said. "Don't you want to see what it is?"

Lucy stopped and looked hard at Raymond. "I think I know what it is," she said in a low voice so that the others wouldn't hear. She pulled the box from her pocket and held it out. "You can have it back if you like."

"No, it's for you, Lucy, really it is. Open it and you'll see."

Lucy broke into a run. "If it's mine, then I can do what I want with it, can't I?" she called over her shoulder. At the convent steps she looked back and saw that Raymond and everyone else had stopped following but were still standing there, looking at her. She'd made a mistake, she now realized, by not letting Raymond play his silly trick on her and then laughing afterward along with the others. She'd missed a chance to be like them, always teasing and playing jokes on each other. Worst of all, Gabriel would hear that she'd been a poor sport, that she probably thought she was better than everybody else.

But it was too late now. Besides, Raymond and the others hardly ever paid any attention or talked to her anymore. All they'd wanted was the chance to trick somebody, and she was probably the only person at Saint Margaret's who didn't already know what the trick was.

Once inside the convent entryway, Lucy lifted the hinged lid of the box very slowly, in case it contained powder that would spill out onto the polished convent floor, or something alive like a worm or a spider. Raymond would know where to find such things, even in winter.

But on the blue-satin lining she found a gold ring with a dark-purple stone lying on a folded paper. Lucy unfolded the paper carefully and in the dim light read the printed words: "To Lucy. Fond regards from Gabriel." She refolded the paper, put it back, and slipped the box in her coat pocket.

Throughout her recitation that day Lucy's mind hummed with the knowledge that Gabriel had sent her a gift. The vision of the shiny gold ring on its square of white, folded paper floated before her eyes.

Lucy didn't open the box again until she got home from school. She went immediately to the attic landing, took the box from her coat pocket, and read the note again. The words were still there. She hadn't imagined them. But when she examined the ring more closely, she saw that although it had come in a proper jewelry box, it was only a child's toy ring, from the dime store.

She had no way of telling if it had been meant as a joke, which would mean that others had guessed how she felt about Gabriel, or if Gabriel had sent it as a special valentine. He might not have expected anyone else to be there when Raymond gave it to her. In fact, now that she thought of it, Raymond *had* seemed curious and genuinely disappointed, as if he didn't know what was inside, when she refused to open the box in front of him.

Lucy went down to the kitchen. "I have to set the table," she told Jeanie, who'd been using the kitchen table to cut out valentines. Jeanie had left everything scattered while she lay on the floor throwing scraps of paper for Min Min, her cat, to chase.

Jeanie went back to sit at the table and started to cut more valentines slowly and carefully with the scissors. "Want to help me?" she asked Lucy. "It's taking a long time, and my hand gets tired."

"Why don't you just punch them out like you're supposed to?"

"Because it makes the edges bumpy. Sometimes they tear, and I need all these valentines because this year I'm giving one to every person in my class."

It was silly of Jeanie to go to such trouble, Lucy was about to say. But the idea that she herself might have received a very special valentine from Gabriel made her say kindly instead, "It will go faster if I push them out; then you can trim the places that are bumpy."

Jeanie hesitated. "All right," she said finally. "Guess what Mother Augusta told me today."

"What?" Lucy was flipping through the pages of Jeanie's book of valentines. They were exactly the same as the ones she'd sent at Jeanie's age, with pictures of animals and funny messages. They seemed especially childish now, compared to a handwritten note and a ring, even if it wasn't a real one.

"Mother Augusta chose me to be in the play on the night of the announcements."

"What announcements?"

"When they announce the winners."

"What winners?"

"You know! The winners of your competition, of course!"

Lucy stared at Jeanie. "I *don't* know, and it isn't *my* competition."

"Mother Augusta said the announcements would be the most important event to happen at Saint Margaret's in a long time," Jeanie said, still busily cutting.

"They're putting on a play? With an audience and everything?"

"Sure. People will be coming from all over. *You* know."

"I *don't* know, so stop saying that!" Lucy said angrily. "It's awful!"

Jeanie had picked up the scissors again and was cutting out the biggest and most elegant valentine from the front cover of the book. Lucy watched impatiently as Jeanie's tongue crept farther and farther down her chin. When she was through, Jeanie said, "I'm giving this one to Mama," and held the valentine up to show Lucy the picture, a bouquet with red hearts in the place of flowers.

Lucy slammed the book shut. "Don't you know

you're supposed to give valentines to boys, not to your mother?"

"Aren't you going to help me?"

"It's time to set the table, so you'll have to clear up this mess."

Jeanie looked at the stove. "Mama hasn't even started fixing supper."

"I want to do it right now and get it over with. Are you sure there's going to be a play?"

"It's called *The Miracle at Lourdes*, and guess what!"

"Just tell me! I don't want to have to guess everything."

"I'm going to play Saint Bernadette."

"Now clear this table," Lucy shouted. "How many times do I have to tell you?"

"Why are you so mad, just because they're putting on a play?"

Later on Lucy was sorry she'd shouted at Jeanie. After all, what had Jeanie done except tell her one more disturbing, completely unexpected piece of news?

9

WHEN LUCY ARRIVED at the school yard the next morning, she saw Madeleine surrounded by a crowd of noisy, excited older girls. With only a quick glance as she went by, Lucy could tell that Madeleine had been showing them a valentine, which they were all admiring.

"Who sent it? Is it from Gabriel?" one girl was asking excitedly as Lucy hurried past.

"I'm not saying," Madeleine said. She was holding the valentine so that only the front could be seen, a huge, bright-red heart with white frilly edging that looked like real lace.

Compared to such an elegant card, which Madeleine had probably received in the mail, having a toy ring handed over in front of anyone who cared to watch seemed childish suddenly, and insulting. Lucy was glad, for once, that she could cross the school yard unnoticed and walk straight into the school without waiting for the bell. She found the classroom empty and even more depressing than usual until she saw, lying on top of her desk, a square envelope large enough to contain a valentine like Madeleine's. When she picked it up it felt empty, but inside she found a small valentine exactly like one she'd seen the night before in Jeanie's book, with a picture of a bear cub dressed in a straw hat and coveralls holding a jar marked HONEY between his paws. Above his head was a red heart with the message "Yours till little bears stop liking honey."

Lucy smiled and turned the valentine over, expecting to find Jeanie's name on the back, but instead there was a huge letter *L* with *ucy* written inside the top loop and *aurence* inside the lower one. She crushed the valentine and the envelope, then smoothed them flat and tore them in half. Tears of fury and disappointment gathered in her eyes, but she forced them back when she heard voices and footsteps on the stairs. She raised the top of her desk and slipped the torn valentine inside just as the class started to file in.

That morning Lucy's hour in the nuns' study crept by even more slowly than usual. She'd had no chance to remove the valentine from her desk without being seen. She tried to concentrate on her reading, but she couldn't stop thinking of the little bear and the huge letter *L* and of her desk being opened, exposing the fact that the brain had received a valentine from the dumbest boy in school.

At noon Lucy stayed in the nuns' study until she was sure that everyone, including Sister Andrew, had left the classroom. She hurried to her desk, opened it, and to her relief found the valentine exactly as she'd left it. She tore it again into smaller pieces, carried them to the coatroom, and stuffed them inside her coat pocket.

She was very hot by the time she got home, but she kept her coat on and stopped in the front hall only long enough to slide the blue-velvet box from its hiding place underneath her pillow. Then she went straight through the kitchen and down the stairs to the cellar. She opened the furnace door and threw the pieces of valentine on the glowing coals. Although the blast of heat stung her eyes and made them water, Lucy watched the pieces of paper turn immediately into flakes that floated upward and disappeared into the blackness of the chimney.

When she threw the box in, it bounced and flew open. The ring fell out, and its stone flashed purple in the firelight. The blue-velvet covering curled up and evaporated, and the thin metal underneath melted and finally collapsed into a shapeless lump.

Using the heavy poker, Lucy piled hot coals over the blob of metal and the place where the ring had fallen, then threw two pieces of firewood on the fire and closed the furnace door.

When she went back upstairs to the kitchen, Mama called from the living room. "Lucy, you'd better eat your soup before it gets cold!"

Lucy sat down, but she couldn't eat. She left the table and went to the living room. Mama was sitting at one end of the sofa, hand sewing some filmy blue cloth. "Why do you still have your coat on?" Mama asked.

Lucy took off her coat, dropped it on the sofa, and sat down next to Mama.

"You haven't finished eating your lunch already?"

"I'm not very hungry today."

"Didn't I hear the furnace door a moment ago?"

"I was just getting rid of some papers. I put more wood on, so you don't have to do it for a while."

"Is something the matter? You look tired."

Lucy shrugged her shoulders. "What are you making?" she asked, touching the cloud of blue fabric in Mama's lap.

"Another costume for Alice." Mama held up one edge of the cloth, which was like a blue veil in front of her face, and smiled through it at Lucy.

"What is it supposed to be?"

"Her mother didn't say."

"It can't be a costume for the Ice Carnival," Lucy said, letting a handful of the cloth cascade from her open hand. "Even Alice would get all tangled up and fall down if she tried to skate in this!" She picked up a wide curve that Mama had finished hemming. "It's like a wing."

"That's a sleeve. All the edges have to be hemmed by hand."

Lucy leaned her head back against the sofa and watched, through half-closed eyes, as the edge of blue cloth moved steadily through Mama's fingers. The long, fine needle flashed in and out steadily. She *was* tired after all, and she felt lost. The dull pain that had been growing inside her sharpened suddenly and made her want to tell Mama about the ring.

114

Lucy picked up a piece of finished hem and brought it close to her eyes. Mama's needle had passed through without leaving a mark, and the thread was completely hidden inside the tiny roll of cloth. "I hope Mrs. Palmer is paying you for all the extra time this is taking?"

"I couldn't charge her for so many hours. But she's brought me steady work, so it's worth it. She's also been sending other people to me for costumes. I don't mind."

"But you should mind!" Lucy said. "You should be paid for your time and for your knowledge too."

"I know," Mama said. "I guess it just isn't very special knowledge."

"That's only because people like Mrs. Palmer don't realize how long it takes and how hard it is to do fine sewing like this. They probably think it just comes naturally, because you're 'French.' Have you ever thought about that?"

"There's such a thing as thinking too much and never getting anything done."

Lucy touched the fabric again. "That's a nice color."

"It's called *Alice blue.* Mrs. Palmer tells me that she chose Alice's name because a few days before Alice was born, she was at a show where a woman danced in a dress this color to an old song called 'Alice Blue Gown.' "

Lucy sighed. "It must be nice to be named after a song and a pretty color instead of some saint who's been dead for hundreds of years."

Mama's needle stopped, then started moving again. "Why don't you just eat something," she said, "and then go back to school?"

For dessert that night Jeanie had baked a valentine cake, which she decorated with white frosting and red candy hearts. Because she hadn't waited long enough for the cake to cool completely before frosting it, the hearts were sliding down the sides by the time she brought it to the table. They left red streaks in the frosting, as if they were bleeding. The twins squealed when they saw the cake and stretched their sticky hands toward it. In spite of the streaks Tessa said, "What a beautiful cake, Jeanie!"

"I got a valentine from every person in my class," Jeanie announced proudly while she cut the cake and held a thick slice of it out to Lucy.

The cake was bright pink on the inside. "I don't want any," Lucy said.

Jeanie's face went blank with disbelief. She continued to hold the plate out to Lucy until Edward reached across the table and took it. "Never mind, Jeanie," he said. "I'm hungry enough to eat two pieces. Lucy's probably too lovesick to eat anything on Valentine's Day."

"What does any of this have to do with Valentine's Day?" Lucy said, waving her hand at the cake, which was growing more and more ragged as Jeanie cut through it. "Saint Valentine was a real saint. It's disgusting how people send silly cards in honor of a martyr who died a horrible death."

"Is that true?" Jeanie asked, looking back and forth from Edward to Lucy. Her mouth was smeared red from eating the candy hearts that fell from each piece. "About the horrible death?"

"Lucy doesn't know," Edward said. "She's only talking. What's really disgusting is that since she entered that scholarship competition, she's been acting as if she's better than everybody else and thinks she knows everything."

Lucy poured herself a cup of tea and raised it to her mouth. But the tea was much too hot to drink. "Edward's the one who thinks he knows everything," she said, watching the steam rising from her cup. "Edward was very quick to say it would be such an honor, but that was only because he knew he wouldn't be the one stuck with having to do anything about it." She'd spoken very calmly, knowing that would annoy Edward much more than if she raised her voice.

Nobody spoke. Mr. Porter was staring hard at his cake plate. Tessa was gathering pink crumbs on a spoon and feeding them to the twins. Lucy's thoughts rushed on. Because of honor, wars started and people died.

Lucy was glad she'd stopped before saying any of these things. Sister Andrew had been teaching her to open her mind to new ideas, no matter how strange they seemed. But lately some of the ideas that entered her mind were more than strange. They were frightening.

"You don't have to know everything to know who Saint Valentine was," she said to Edward. "You can look it up."

"I'm certainly not going to look it up," Edward said.

Lucy was relieved. She'd only been guessing about Saint Valentine, and if she was wrong, Edward would never let her forget. She smiled at him and held up both her hands, like a soldier surrendering. Edward laughed.

"It's probably in the dictionary," Jeanie said, and before Lucy could stop her, she'd left the room. She came back a moment later carrying the open dictionary. "Here it is. 'Valentine, Saint,'" Jeanie read slowly. "'Bishop of Terni, martyred third century A.D. Celebrated February 14.'"

"I hope that ends the discussion," Mama said.

"You were right, Lucy," Jeanie said in an awed tone of voice. "Some people at school say you've memorized the whole dictionary. Is that true? Do you really know everything that's in here?"

"Of course I don't! I was guessing, that's all." Lucy pulled the corners of her mouth far down in a comically stupid expression and looked over at Edward.

Everyone laughed. It was the first time she and Edward had ended an argument like this, with a joke, instead of yelling at each other. It was the first time also that Lucy hadn't minded hearing that people at Saint Margaret's were talking about her. Even though the rumor about the work she'd been doing all this time wasn't true, it meant that she was admired for doing it. It might even explain why Gabriel would want to send her a note through Raymond, instead of giving it to her himself.

From now on, Lucy decided, she'd go outside like the rest of the class after school and join in the talking and joking. Now that she'd become a kind of outsider, the jokes would probably be about her at first, but she'd laugh and show that she was the same as everyone else and that she belonged. Besides, after that valentine, she wanted to avoid spending time with Laurence Constantine.

Sister Andrew nodded in agreement when Lucy explained that she wanted to spend a few minutes outdoors at the end of each day. "Laurence will be disappointed, of course," Sister Andrew told her, "but you *are* beginning to look a little worn."

When Lucy went outside that day immediately after class, she saw Gabriel climbing the rocky path with Raymond and Madeleine. When they reached the top, they turned in front of the church steps and disappeared in the direction of Madeleine's house. Since Madeleine had positioned herself, as if automatically, to walk between the two boys, it seemed clear that Gabriel and Raymond were walking her home from school, and that they now did so every day.

Without them, there was no noisy gathering in the school yard on that day or on most of the days that followed. Whenever Lucy had to wait for Sister Andrew, she climbed the path alone and waited inside Saint Margaret's Church. If she saw Madeleine, Raymond, and Gabriel, she stayed far behind them and entered by the wide granite steps and through the huge, ornately carved front door. The door was heavy and closed slowly, with a final push of air that sounded exactly, in the vast emptiness of the church, like a ghostly sigh.

Lucy would have preferred to go into the

church by the side door, which was the usual size and easy to open. But as Gabriel and the others always went in that direction, she was afraid they might see her and think she'd been following them. She had completely lost her resolve to approach them and join in their conversation.

She always sat in the very last row without ever kneeling or praying. She could see, at the other end of the dimly lit, silent church, the red sanctuary lamp flickering in the distance. The lamp was suspended on a long chain from the ceiling above the altar, but as the chain was invisible from so far away, the flame seemed to be hanging, miraculously, in midair. One day, after she'd been staring at the flame for a long time, Lucy was reminded of a picture in her prayer book that showed tongues of fire appearing above the heads of the apostles on Pentecost. But almost nothing else entered her mind in the time she spent staring into the vastness of the empty church, waiting for the minutes to pass.

One day a nun appeared briefly from behind the altar and arranged the altar cloths and flowers. Lucy tried to imagine it was Claire, but the thought that Claire might ever become such a remote, mysterious, silently moving figure made her feel more alone and hollow than ever.

Only one other person, Madeleine's mother,

ever came into the church in the late afternoon while Lucy was there. Like Lucy, Mrs. Larose always arrived by the front entrance, but the sigh of the heavy door when it closed behind her was the only way Lucy had of knowing that someone had just come in. Then, unlike Lucy, Madeleine's mother always walked down the center aisle all the way to the front, knelt down, and bowed her head in prayer. Everyone knew that Mrs. Larose went to church each day to pray for a miracle that would cure her son, Madeleine's older brother, who had been born severely retarded and lived in an institution.

Lucy usually left soon after Mrs. Larose arrived. It felt wrong to be sitting in church, doing nothing, with someone who had really come to pray. She would have liked to pray for a miracle too, one that would bring back her normal life, the life she'd been having before the Christmas vacation when she and Gabriel had talked after school almost every day. It wasn't true, in spite of what Jeanie had told her about the dictionary, that people at Saint Margaret's had been discussing her with admiration. On the contrary—everyone Lucy knew, including Jeanie, had lately become very busy and preoccupied, so she felt, more and more, that she was invisible.

10

IN THE PERFECT stillness of the nuns' study Lucy sometimes fell asleep with her head on the table and woke up with her neck stiff and sore. At home she lay down on the sofa every day after school and had to be woken several times before coming to the table for supper.

"Are you getting enough sleep at night?" Mama asked her one day.

"She can sleep in my room if she wants," Edward said.

"I don't want to sleep in your stuffy little room," Lucy snapped back.

"I was only trying to help," Edward told Mama. "It's all right with me if she prefers to sleep in a noisy, drafty hallway."

"You only want to sleep there so nobody will notice what time you come in at night," Lucy said.

As time went on, Lucy regretted her refusal of Edward's offer. She was finding it harder and harder to sleep at night, and when she did fall asleep, she had nightmares. She dreamed again and again that she was walking through a troop train, looking for Victor. The aisles of the train were so tightly packed with soldiers in uniform that it was almost impossible to get through. From the back all the soldiers looked alike, and each time she thought she'd found Victor, the soldier would turn around and she'd see the face of a stranger. Sometimes the soldier smiled at her mistake. For some reason the smile, no matter how friendly, was always terrifying.

The entire family had once gone to the station to meet a troop train that Victor was traveling on. Like the one in Lucy's dream, the real train had also been packed with soldiers, all wearing identical lumpy, dull-green uniforms. The train windows were filled with soldiers leaning out and waving. And just as in her dream, the soldiers all looked so much alike that for a long time no one in the family was able to find Victor. People were running frantically back and forth alongside the train, looking up at the windows and crashing into each other.

After they'd searched the entire length of the train without finding Victor, Mama said, "He's not there!" Then she burst into tears. Lucy saw Papa's face crumple for an instant, as though he might start to cry too.

The soldiers on the train were on their way overseas, but no one knew that for sure. "Troop movements are a military secret," Victor had told them in his latest letter, but somehow everybody in town knew that the train would be coming through on that day. Lucy was standing at the very edge of the crowded platform when a soldier walked up to her and said, "Hello, Lucy!" She stared at him, wondering how this stranger knew her name, before realizing that the soldier was Victor.

When Lucy woke up after a bad dream, she was afraid to go back to sleep. To keep herself awake, she watched the dark above the stairs for the rectangle of pale-gray light to come through the landing window, which meant that dawn had finally come.

Victor had not died in a battle, as they'd all been so afraid would happen. He'd been wounded and taken to a hospital. He was very lucky, his last letter had said, because he wasn't badly wounded and had been given a job as a motorcycle messenger while he finished recovering. Victor had died soon afterward when his motorcycle collided with a truck on a narrow country road. The letter from his captain described Victor as "a brave, good-humored young soldier," and Lucy wondered what Victor would have thought about being called brave.

"You won't do anything foolish, will you?" Papa had said to him when they were saying good-bye.

"I have no plans to become a hero!" Victor's angry reply had surprised everyone, though no one said anything. "I'll just do as I'm told. Nobody I know wants to do anything more than come home." Victor had talked very little on his last visits home. He'd acted impatient to get back to his friends in the army, who seemed more like his family now.

Victor also ate very little. "Aren't you hungry?" Lucy asked him. "Mama's been cooking all your favorite dishes, you know."

She'd meant only to tease him, but Victor looked at her thoughtfully for a long time, then answered seriously, "I know she has. It's almost as if I've learned to like army food better. You won't tell Mama, will you?"

"I won't," Lucy said resentfully. "You don't have to remind me." Victor laughed suddenly then and ruffled her hair. She resented that even more. It was the kind of annoying adult gesture that Victor never made toward her, and she'd moved her head roughly out of his reach.

The moment the light began to appear above the landing, Lucy usually fell into a deep sleep. She slept through the noise of breakfast, of doors slamming, even of hurrying footsteps on the stairs above her bed. If she heard them, the sounds of people getting up helped to lock her more tightly in peaceful, dreamless sleep.

Mama was sewing until late every night. Dozens of Ice Carnival costumes were hanging, half finished, from the living-room curtain rods, and their spangles and bright colors made the faded carpet and furniture seem more drab than ever. As soon as the twins were asleep, Tessa came down to help. She and Mama seldom spoke while they worked together, because there was no door between the living room and the front hall, where Lucy was supposed to be asleep.

A few days before the opening of the Ice Carnival, Mama remarked to Lucy, "I'll be glad when I've finished those costumes. I'm sure the noise is keeping you awake at night." But Lucy knew she'd miss lying in bed listening to the whir of the sewing machine. Even the high-pitched, pan-icky noise the sewing-machine needle made as it raced along a seam made her feel normal and safe.

On Saturday morning, the day after the opening of the Ice Carnival, Lucy stopped by to see Alice on her way to school.

"She's still asleep," Mrs. Palmer said, and handed Lucy two pink cards. "These are com-plimentary reserved passes for tonight's show. One is for you. The other is for your mother. The costumes are beautiful, and I'm sure she'll want to see the results of all her hard work."

Most years there hadn't been enough money even for ordinary tickets to the Ice Carnival, and Lucy hadn't expected to go. She knew she ought to be thrilled at the chance to sit in reserved seats, which were closest to the ice, and to see Alice's performance. But she was sure that watching Alice in the Ice Carnival would make her own life seem unbearably drab.

Mama had put the sewing machine away and was vacuuming the living room when Lucy showed her the Carnival passes. "I was hoping to go to bed early tonight for a change," Mama said, bending over to pick up a strip of sparkling cloth. "Jeanie wants me to save these scraps for her.

Take her with you to the Carnival. She'll enjoy it much more than I would."

"I don't feel like going," Lucy said. "I think I'll go to bed early too."

Mama switched off the vacuum cleaner. "At your age you shouldn't be too exhausted to take advantage of a chance like this," she told Lucy. "I want you to go and enjoy yourself. Forget about studying and books for tonight."

"You should go with Jeanie. Don't you want to see how your costumes turned out?"

"I've seen enough of those costumes. Besides, most of them are so short and tight, I'm afraid they won't stay on. I'd be worrying too much." Mama laughed.

The passes Mrs. Palmer had given Lucy were for seats in the first row, next to the ice. "We won't miss a thing from here!" Jeanie said happily as she wriggled her arms out of her coat sleeves. She rubbed her glasses extra hard with her handkerchief and put them on, then leaned forward and placed both arms on top of the barrier.

The show started with a blast of loud, rhythmic music that seemed to pour down from the darkness above the ice as skaters of all sizes spilled out from behind a curved screen covering the entrance. They were dressed in costumes made of green, orange, and yellow cloth that had taken

Mama hours to cut and stitch together in the shapes of leaves and flowers.

"There's Alice, the one in the middle!" Jeanie pointed. Alice looked taller, and much older. Her head was wrapped in a red turban with a straw hat on top. The hat had a wide, turned-up brim filled with brightly colored artificial fruit. "Alice!" Jeanie called, and leaped to her feet. Someone shouted "Down in front!" but Jeanie was too excited to hear, and Lucy had to pull her back into her seat.

For the next hour Jeanie hardly moved, not even when skaters sped past only a few inches from her face. Lucy was happy to be there with Jeanie, but by the intermission her head was pounding from so much movement, color, and music. "Let's go home," she said to Jeanie. "It's probably almost over anyway."

"No it isn't," Jeanie said. "Look!" The curved entrance screen had been moved to one side. Two ice machines rolled onto the ice and began scraping and watering it. "They wouldn't be doing that if it was almost over. I brought money for hot chocolate. I'll buy you some too, Lucy."

When Lucy and Jeanie came back, the machines were gone. The ice surface gleamed like a pool of still water, reflecting every light and color, including the movement of people returning to their seats.

While people in the audience were still turned around in their seats, talking to each other, the lights suddenly went out. After a few seconds of shocked silence and complete darkness, they gradually came on again, only now they were blue. They made the air above the ice look thick, like blue smoke. Music floated down, as though hundreds of violins had started playing in the darkness above—the long slow notes of a waltz that grew louder, then paused. A shaft of white light shone down on the curved screen—and on Alice, who had come out, unseen, and was standing in front of it.

Gasps and whispers of surprise swept through the audience. Instead of the usual short, tight skating costume, Alice was draped in the long blue dress that Mama had been hemming on Valentine's Day. The violin music started again, this time with a chorus singing "In your sweet little Alice blue gown..." as Alice started moving slowly across the blue ice, bending and turning with the music, the circle of light following her.

Except for a sparkly blue flower on one side, Alice's head was bare, but the rest of her was covered by the dress. Its full, deep folds floated

131

around her, attached only at her wrists and neck with silver cords so thin that they were visible only as a flashing sliver of light. When Alice picked up speed, the cloth pushed tight against her body and fluttered behind her. When she raised her arms, the wide sleeves filled with air and were swept back. Underneath her feet Alice's shadow moved along the ice surface like a giant blue moth folding and unfolding its wings.

"She looks naked!" Jeanie whispered.

"Don't be so silly! She's got tights on underneath," Lucy said.

"Shhh!" Several people hissed disapprovingly, as if to silence someone who had been talking in church.

Alice had practiced hard for weeks, Lucy knew, but she seemed to glide as easily as a bird flying through air. It wasn't until she passed very close that Lucy saw the sparkle of sweat on her forehead. On her face was the same concentrated expression that Lucy had observed on that bright Saturday morning from the bathroom window. And the audience was just as silent and entranced, watching her, as Edward had been.

With the last long note of music, Alice vanished behind the curved screen. The blue lights went out. A single beam of gold-colored light cut through the dark, and the air vibrated suddenly with organ music playing "Ave Maria." In the circle of gold light, Alice reappeared with a lighted candelabrum in each hand, high above her head.

Jeanie sat up, and Lucy heard her own shocked intake of breath at seeing someone carrying lighted candles and skating to hymn music. But Alice wasn't actually skating. After one hard push, she was circling the ice in a single, motionless glide close to the edge, followed by the golden shaft of light. Only her fluttering dress moved, except for the candle flames, which dropped tiny sparks behind her into the darkness. Alice's hair glowed brightly under the candlelight, but the gold spotlight had turned her blue dress dark bronze, like a statue's.

Alice completed the circle, then turned and came to a stop at the center of the ice. The gold light went out, and for a few seconds the candle flames were tiny points of flickering light in total, velvety blackness. The regular white spotlight came on, and two of the youngest skaters, a boy and a girl, skated to either side of Alice. She lowered her arms and carefully handed a candelabrum to each of the children, who then blew out the candles and carried them away.

Alice raised her hands to the side so that the sleeves opened like blue wings, and bowed her head. The audience started to applaud, a few at a time, as if afraid to break the spell. The applause grew until the air of the Ice Palace shook with a deafening mixture of shouts, whistles, and stamping of feet. Someone tossed a bouquet of red roses onto the ice. Alice skated in a wide curve past the flowers, picked them up without stopping, and waved them at the cheering crowd. Row after row of people stood up as Alice went past until she disappeared behind the screen. The applause continued even after all the lights had been turned back on.

Lucy and Jeanie walked most of the way home in silence. "I didn't think they'd be allowed to play a hymn in an ice carnival, did you?" Jeanie said after a while.

"Why not? Anyway, 'Ave Maria' is *not* a hymn."

"It's a prayer, isn't it? Doesn't that make it even more holy?"

Lucy didn't answer. She didn't feel like talking.

"Well *I* don't think they should. Anyway not with Alice looking naked like that."

"She wasn't naked!"

"If Father Martin ever finds out, he'll say that people shouldn't go to the Ice Carnival. It *was* sort of holy though, don't you think?"

"Yes," Lucy had to agree. "It was."

11

ALICE'S TRIUMPHANT performance and the colors and sounds of the Ice Carnival echoed in Lucy's head and kept her half-awake through most of the night. She woke up too late for the early Mass, which was especially for schoolchildren, and had to attend the later, longer one. When she came home, Jeanie was outside building a snow house with her friends. She ran to meet Lucy and told her breathlessly, "Father Martin talked about you in church today."

"That's impossible," Lucy said, bending over

to pick up Min Min, who had run behind Jeanie, lifting his paws high in the snow.

"I didn't hear him myself," Jeanie said, petting the cat's black fur as he lay purring in Lucy's arms. "Somebody else told me it was you he was talking about. I only heard him talking about Lent. He didn't say your name. I know I would have heard that."

Jeanie turned to go back to her friends. Min Min jumped down and followed her. "I'm sure Father Martin doesn't know me or my name," Lucy called after her.

When Lucy came in the front door, Mr. Porter was standing in the doorway to the kitchen, talking with Mama. He stopped, turned, and looked at Lucy. "Good morning, or should I say good afternoon?" he said with an embarrassed little laugh, then hurried up the stairs.

"What was Mr. Porter talking to you about, and why did he rush off like that?"

"I suppose it's because we'd just been talking about you."

Lucy had taken off her coat. She threw it on the floor. "*Everybody*'s talking about me behind my back!" she yelled. "Even Claire's been discussing me with Sister Andrew. Jeanie says Father Martin mentioned me in his sermon this morning. I don't think there's anybody left who doesn't have something to say, not even Mr. Porter, and he hardly ever says anything!"

"All he said was that he's heard you talking in your sleep at night when he comes in late. Sometimes he thinks you're calling someone's name."

To hide her dismay, Lucy bent over and picked up her coat. Had she spoken Gabriel's name while she was asleep? "I don't see what the fuss is about," she said. "Jeanie does it all the time. So do a lot of other people, maybe even Mr. Porter, except that he sleeps in a room with a door he can close so that nobody can spy on him."

"He wasn't spying on you. He's been working late, that's all. He tells me that you seem to be calling Victor. I'm glad he spoke to me. I've been saying for weeks that you're not sleeping well, and now I want you to move into Edward's room and let him sleep on the hall bed."

"Why should I have to move to Edward's room just because Mr. Porter can't mind his own business?" Lucy shouted, then lowered her voice when she saw the look of shock on Mama's face. "All I want," she said very quietly, "is to be left alone."

"On the contrary, you've been alone far too much lately, it seems to me," Mama said as Lucy sat down to a very late breakfast.

Afterward she went into the dining room, now Mama's bedroom, and lay down. She was exhausted, but the longer she waited to fall asleep, the more her mind churned with thoughts that kept her awake. It was Mr. Porter's fault that she'd screamed at Mama. He was always so polite, but a truly polite person would have ignored what she said while she was asleep. After all, it was only because Mama had to rent out a room that strangers like him could walk past Lucy's bed while she was sleeping.

She refused to move to Edward's room, which was a mess from floor to ceiling. Just thinking of it was suffocating. Lucy pushed aside the hot comforter and sat up. She slid her feet into her shoes and went out to the front hall. A moment later she was dressed in her coat and boots and on her way down the porch steps. When she reached the bottom she turned right, in the direction of the rocks and the lake. She couldn't stay inside a minute longer, but she didn't feel like taking her usual Sunday walk either. If she walked through the town, she'd have to see houses and cars and people, and the only thing she knew for sure was that she had to get away from everything and everybody.

The sky was covered with low clouds that made the air warm and heavy. She'd left her coat unbuttoned, and when she reached the rocks and had to climb, its corners hung down and caused her to stumble. Her feet sank through the slushy snow in the deep, narrow spaces between rocks, and she had to pull hard to get free. By the time she reached the edge of the cliff above the lake, Lucy's stockings were soaked and her feet numb with cold.

The snow at the edge of the cliff had melted or blown away and left a clear line of brown grass where the land dropped. Lucy stood close to the rim and looked down. Far below, between the face of the cliff and the frozen lake surface, a narrow channel of black, open water had opened. She could hear the waves lapping faintly against the smooth pink wall.

The water of her recitation poem would also have looked calm, she thought, after the sleigh and the people had disappeared. The poem didn't say how long the family watched the water rise, how many minutes passed before it finally closed over their heads. It didn't say either whether they drowned, or died first from the cold. Cold was supposed to be the easiest way to die, like sinking into a deep, pleasant sleep.

The water at the base of the cliff was silky, and not black after all, but a mixture of brown, like dark chocolate, and very deep blue. If she were to step off the edge now, she'd slice cleanly through it instead of sinking slowly, struggling and thrashing, as the people in the poem had done. There wouldn't be time to feel the terror they must have felt when they heard the ice crack as it gave way beneath them and saw the dark water opening.

It would be so much simpler to take just one step, then drop past the smooth face of the rock, first through air, then through water. The water would close over her head right away. In a second or two the surface would be just as smooth and the waves as gentle as they were now.

That night Lucy was awakened by a hand squeezing her shoulder. "Wake up now, and go back to bed," Mama said. Lucy opened her eyes and saw through the dimness that Mama's face was close to hers. "Go back to your bed, Lucy," Mama repeated. They were in Tessa's room, and Lucy was sitting in the rocking chair next to the window. A narrow band of cold air blowing in across the windowsill made Lucy remember how cold the chair had felt through her nightgown when she sat down in it. The door of Tessa's room was dark with people. Under the hall light was a man's head with black, uncombed hair and the shoulders of striped pajamas, and it wasn't until he spoke that she recognized Mr. Porter. "Will you need help to take her downstairs?" he said.

From the doorway came Tessa's voice. "She shouldn't walk down the stairs by herself. I think you're not supposed to wake up a sleepwalker, but when I saw her sitting there in the dark, it gave me such a fright!"

Lucy stood up. The chair wobbled unsteadily. "You don't have to say 'her' and 'she' as if I wasn't here," she said, pushing between Edward and Tessa, who were blocking the door. Mr. Porter stepped far back to let her pass, as if afraid of her. Lucy went down the dark stairs. Mama followed close behind, then slipped ahead to straighten the blankets on Lucy's bed. She held them back until Lucy had lain down and curled up on her side with her face to the wall. While Mama pulled the blankets over her, Lucy kept her eyes closed and lay very still, as though she'd fallen asleep again right away.

But she was wide awake. In the middle of the night and without knowing it, she had gotten out of bed, walked up the stairs, and sat in the rocking chair in Tessa's room. In her long white flannel nightgown, she must have looked exactly like a ghost. It was no wonder that Tessa had been so frightened to wake up and see someone sitting there by the window.

But Lucy had frightened herself even more. What if she'd walked out the front door, which was only a few feet from her bed? No one would have seen her. She might have retraced her steps all the way to the edge of the cliff. She might have fallen into the lake and disappeared forever without anyone knowing what had happened.

In the upstairs hall Tessa, Edward, Mama, and Mr. Porter were still talking. "That settles it," Lucy heard Mama say. "From now on she must sleep in your room, Edward. Next Saturday, and no later, the two of you will trade places. Meantime, we'll just have to keep an eye on her."

Before going back to bed, Mama spread extra blankets over Lucy, but Lucy lay awake for a very long time, shivering with cold.

12

SHROVE TUESDAY, the week following the Ice Carnival, marked the last day before Lent, the only time in the school year when classes at Saint Margaret's stopped an hour early to have a party. Each room held its own celebration, with everyone bringing a special treat to share with the rest of the class before giving up desserts and candies for the next forty days. When Lucy came home from school the day before, Jeanie had just finished icing the cupcakes she'd baked for her class party. They were in fluted paper cups and iced in pink, green, and yellow. Jeanie placed a walnut half carefully at the center of each cupcake. "Don't you think it's a nice finishing touch?" she asked Lucy.

The cupcakes' warm, delicious smell when she came in had made Lucy feel faint. Would Sister Andrew let her stay in the nuns' study or go home, she wondered, instead of going to the party? " 'Finishing touch,' " she repeated sarcastically. But when she saw the proud expression vanish from Jeanie's face, she said quickly, "I wish I had something as nice to take to the eighth-grade party." She didn't mean it. Last year, at the seventh-grade party, she'd been one of the few who brought something homemade. Madeleine's mother had sent a huge box of chocolates, individually wrapped in gold and silver paper.

"You can take some of these," Jeanie said. "I'm not supposed to take this many anyway."

Like everyone else at Saint Margaret's, Lucy had looked forward each year to the Shrove Tuesday party. It was like an island of color and fun in the long, dark stretch of time between Christmas and Easter. But this year, after arriving late from the nuns' study, she felt awkward and out of place. Everyone was already wandering among the desks, talking and carrying paper cups of the watery fruit punch that the convent contributed to the parties every year. The only person in the room she felt she could talk with was Claire, who had come to school just for the party. But Claire was in a corner, her back to the classroom, in deep discussion with Sister Andrew.

Sister Andrew's desk had been cleared of books and covered with sheets of clean paper. The treats had been set out, including Jeanie's cupcakes, which were all gone except one. Laurence pushed his long arm through the crowd and took it.

"These are good!" he said to Lucy. "Did you make them?"

"My little sister made them," Lucy answered. She'd hardly spoken to Laurence since the day before Valentine's Day, and he'd never asked why she'd stopped helping with his lessons. Now, she found that her anger over the valentine had dissolved completely. She was grateful to him, in fact, for speaking to her after she'd been ignoring him all these weeks. "Then you're not the only one in the family who's talented," Laurence said.

Someone had dropped one of the fluted papers. Lucy picked it up, carried it to the wastebasket at the front of the room, and stayed there, brushing crumbs from her hands and wishing the party would end.

She could hear marching music coming up from the first floor. Sister Isabel's first-grade pupils had made animal masks out of paper and flour paste and must be having a parade. The eighth-grade party had been very quiet so far, and was even quieter now that the food and almost all the punch were gone. Lucy wondered for the first time which of the nuns made the punch each year. After the first day she'd gone straight into the convent without ringing the doorbell, and so hadn't seen again the little nun with the red hands. But Lucy could picture her mixing gallons of sugar and water and fruit juice, without ever tasting a drop of it.

Madeleine, Gabriel, and Raymond were in the middle of the room, surrounded by a large group. Raymond was talking and waving his hands in the air, causing bursts of laughter.

"Hey Lucy!" he called out suddenly. "Come over here!" The group turned at the same time toward Lucy. They had the same smiling curiosity on their faces as on the day they'd watched Raymond hand her the box with the toy ring inside it. But Gabriel was there too this time, and Lucy thought she could see the same half-smiling, expectant look on his face.

"Come on, Lucy!" Raymond coaxed. "There's something we want to ask you."

Lucy moved forward hesitantly. Several people stepped aside and made room for her on top of a desk. Gabriel hadn't moved from where he was sitting, on the opposite desk across the narrow aisle.

"We want you to tell us how it feels to be the subject of a sermon," Raymond said.

"I don't know what you're talking about," Lucy spoke carefully, distracted by Gabriel's presence.

"I'm talking about last Sunday."

"What do you mean?" Lucy asked nervously.

Raymond laughed. "You weren't at the nine-o'clock Mass last Sunday? Father Martin's sermon was about Lent. He said we must all make sacrifices and give up the things we like best," Raymond intoned, lifting his eyes comically toward the ceiling. " 'One young person in our parish has taken on the burden of study, is devoting hours, days, weeks' "—Raymond was holding his hand out toward Lucy—" 'for the honor of her school, her family. . . .' " All around Lucy people were laughing loudly at Raymond's imitation. "How does it feel to be the subject of a sermon, Lucy?" Raymond asked again.

Lucy glanced quickly across the aisle. "I guess you weren't there," Gabriel explained. "We knew he was talking about you, even though he didn't actually say your name." Lucy recognized Jeanie's words. The faces around her blurred together as several people spoke to her at once.

"Father Martin meant *you*, all right," Madeleine

said. "He said so when he came to our house that night for supper. He also told my parents some very interesting things about Sister Andrew. He said that if she wasn't a nun, she'd be called Doctor." Madeleine had lowered her voice, so that everyone had to lean forward to listen. Gabriel's head was so close to Lucy's that his hair brushed her cheek.

"She's a Doctor of Pedagogy," Madeleine explained. "That's the science of teaching."

"I didn't know there was such a thing as a science of teaching," Lucy said. "I thought—"

"She went to a university in France." Lucy was grateful for the interruption. She didn't want to talk, or think about anything except that she was sitting at the very center of the group, right next to Gabriel. "She had to leave France because of the war," Madeleine was saying, "and she makes speeches at teachers' conferences. She's even written a book about teaching. But you probably know all that, Lucy."

"No, I didn't." Lucy looked around at the circle of waiting faces. "We talk mostly about what I'm studying, language and writing, things like that." After all these weeks of not mentioning her work to anyone except Claire, it felt like breaking a vow of silence.

"If Sister Andrew is so important," someone

asked, "what's she doing here in Rockford, in a school like Saint Margaret's?"

"Father Martin says she's probably writing something while she's here," Madeleine said. "I wonder what it's about."

"She spends a lot of time with Lucy," Raymond said. "Maybe she's writing about her."

"She spends a lot of time with Laurence, too," someone else said. "Maybe she'll write a book about both of them. Lucy and Laurence."

Everybody laughed, including Gabriel. But Lucy couldn't laugh. The remark had connected her name with Laurence's in almost exactly the same way as his horrible valentine. He must have shown it around before leaving it on her desk.

Lucy started to get down from the desk, but Gabriel put out his hand to stop her. "Sister Andrew picked you out of all the others to train for this competition," he said quietly. "That's really something, isn't it?"

"*I* don't think so," Lucy said. After the joke about her and Laurence, the talk all around them had moved to other subjects.

"Think you'll make it all the way to the finals?" Gabriel asked, more loudly. Several people turned toward them.

"You're making it sound just like a hockey game," Lucy said, smiling in spite of herself.

"It's a contest, and you're in training," he said seriously. "So—do you think you'll make it to the finals?" Gabriel asked again.

Lucy hesitated. What would Gabriel think, she wondered, if she answered, truthfully, that most of the time she was only pretending to study for the exams, that she sometimes did nothing at all in the nuns' study but sleep and look out of the window?

"If you make it to the finals," Gabriel said suddenly, "I'll take you to a movie to celebrate."

Raymond said, "We heard that!" He put one arm around Lucy's shoulders and the other around Gabriel, who leaned forward and said to Lucy, "Just make it to the finals."

Lucy sat without moving in the midst of excited comments and cheering following Gabriel's words. The noise was so loud that Claire and Sister Andrew stopped talking for a moment and turned in her direction.

When the bell rang a few minutes later, the whole class left at once except Lucy and Claire.

Sister Andrew told Lucy to go home. "I'm canceling our session," she said. "One day less will make no difference."

"I'd prefer to stay and work," Lucy said. Although she'd wanted to leave while the others were still outside, Gabriel's promise had made her regret deeply all the hours of study she'd already wasted. If she worked extra hard from now on, she might still have a chance to place first in the regionals. Gabriel and everyone else thought that she'd been working hard all this time to train herself, like a hockey player, and that's exactly what she was determined to do from now on.

"You've had no time off," Sister Andrew said.

"Come on, Lucy. We can walk home together," Claire said eagerly.

When Claire and Lucy walked out the front door, they were immediately surrounded by people who wanted to talk about Gabriel's invitation and about Lucy's chances of winning. When Lucy started toward home with Claire, Raymond called after them, "What are you giving up for Lent, Lucy?"

"I always give up going to the movies," Lucy called back without thinking, then felt her face get hot. But from the loud burst of laughter that followed, it was clear that her answer, like everything else she'd said for the past few minutes, was considered funny and clever.

When they were walking alone, Claire asked Lucy, "How does it feel to have the nicest boy in the whole school ask to take you somewhere?"

"He didn't really ask me," Lucy said cautiously. "He said he would if I win the regionals. He probably knows I don't have much of a chance." She was too excited about Gabriel's invitation, which she still couldn't quite believe, to discuss it with anyone, even Claire.

The following Saturday, after agreeing to do all the work herself, Lucy moved into Edward's room. It was small and rectangular, with barely enough space for the metal cot and a small desk and chair. Above one side of the bed a narrow window looked out onto the brick wall of the house next door, only a few feet away. As the bricks absorbed most of the light, the room stayed dim throughout the day.

After clearing out Edward's things, Lucy scrubbed the floor and every piece of furniture with a hard brush, soap, and hot water. When she finished, the paint on the bed, desk, and chair seemed even more chipped and stained, and she wished she could repaint everything. She wanted the room to be as shiny and spotless as the nuns' study.

She remade the bed with clean sheets and covered it with one of the thin white summer bedspreads. While she was running her hands over the bed to smooth out the creases, Jeanie came in with a plaster statue of the Virgin cradled on one arm, like a doll. Lucy had received the statue as a prize for scholarship in the fourth grade. The Virgin's face was gentle beneath its blue veil, but at the bottom edge of her long white robe her bare foot could be seen, crushing a coiled, brownish-green snake.

While Jeanie and Lucy had been sharing the room that Tessa and the twins were now using, Jeanie had become very attached to the statue and had kept it decorated in spring and summer with small bunches of flowers—always arranged at the base, Lucy noticed, so that they hid the snake. After Jeanie had started sleeping in the dining room with Mama, Lucy had let her take the statue.

"You want this back now?" Jeanie said, holding the statue out to Lucy.

"Yes. Put it on the desk."

"You can have this, too." Jeanie placed a red glass candle holder with a white votive candle inside it in front of the statue. "The candle is blessed, and the red glass looks pretty when it's lit."

"Thanks," Lucy said, pushing the bedspread far under the pillow with her hand to make a sharp, neat crease.

"Everything is so clean in here," Jeanie said, sniffing the air. "It smells like soap. And it's so cold, too." She went over to the statue, patted its veiled head, and left.

Lucy covered the scarred desk with a clean pillowcase. When she picked up the statue, she noticed that Jeanie had fastened a scrap of cloth over the blue plaster veil, and recognized the filmy blue fabric of Alice's skating costume.

Every Saturday afternoon from then on, Lucy lit the candle in the red candle holder and sat down at the desk. She watched the flame and imagined herself going into the Arc with Gabriel. She was sure that she wanted to meet him at the theater, so that he wouldn't see where she lived. But she wasn't sure if she wanted them to sit alone or with other people from Saint Margaret's. It would be wonderful not to have Raymond or Madeleine around, but if they were there at least she wouldn't have to worry about running out of things to talk about.

Lucy looked forward at the end of each day to returning to Edward's room. It was always exactly the same, perfectly neat and clean and full of cold, pure air from the window, which she always left wide open. Once inside and with the door closed, she felt a long way from everything, as if the room were a ship waiting to carry her away.

13

SUDDENLY EVERYBODY at school knew Lucy. All the nuns called her by name, and Father Martin smiled when he saw her at the communion table. One day after Sister Isabel had sprained her ankle, Sister Rose asked Lucy to take charge of the first grade for the rest of the day. From then on, whenever the little first-grade girls saw Lucy walking across the school yard, they ran to meet her and fought over whose turn it was to hold her hand as they walked along with her.

In the late afternoon a shaft of sunlight now entered the nuns' study through a corner of the window. Each day it came a little earlier and moved farther along the bookshelves. On most days, once the sun had made the room bright, she found it impossible to go on studying and stood on a chair to look out the window at the wooded hills in the distance. Now when she walked through the woods on Sunday after-noons, the earth was still damp and cool under her feet, but most of the snow had melted. Against the sky she could see tiny leaf buds form-ing on the bare branches, and from the nuns' study window the hills seemed covered in a red and pale-green veil.

If she stood on her toes and looked straight down, she could see the boys' yard, where the plank walls of the skating rink had been removed and the older boys played baseball after school. But Gabriel and Raymond seldom played, and she wondered why.

One day she stood in front of the two pictures of farmers and examined them closely. She'd seen them every day since the morning she'd first come to the nuns' study, but she realized now for the first time something very important about the one called *The Angelus*. The angel of the prayer was named Gabriel, and the picture seemed to contain a special, secret message revealed only to her, that only she would understand.

Lucy still went to church each day after school, but instead of just sitting, she prayed for success in the regional exams. God would approve, she told herself, because she was asking for something that everybody else wanted too.

Sometimes, in the silent church, Lucy heard shouting and pounding noises coming from the parish hall in the church basement. She wondered at first what they were, then remembered Father Martin's many sermons about the church needing repairs. They must finally be under way, she thought, and from then on she ignored the sounds and concentrated on her prayers.

Lucy's reciting improved, but no matter how hard she tried, it was still far from good. No matter how well she performed in the written parts of the exam, she had no chance of placing first if she gave a poor recitation.

At night, while she lay in Edward's room waiting to fall asleep, passages from the day's reading and rules of grammar she'd memorized tumbled together inside her head. Sometimes a better answer to one of Sister Andrew's questions, which were growing harder all the time, flashed into her mind, and she kept pencil and paper on the chair next to the bed. Writing her thoughts down was sometimes the only way to free her mind of them and go to sleep. When she finally did fall asleep, she often dreamed that she was reading page after page of print that flowed before her eyes like an endless river of words.

Although her sleep was just as disturbed in Edward's room as it had been in the front hall, Lucy was never tired and had stopped falling asleep in the nuns' study. She got up early every morning to attend Mass, then went straight to the classroom to help Sister Andrew prepare for the day. It became her regular job to write the daily homework assignment and school announcements on the blackboard. One morning the class came in when she hadn't quite finished. Raymond stopped as he passed by and read aloud what she was writing. Gabriel stood next to him.

"You're a mean teacher, Lucy!" Raymond said in a loud whisper. "Couldn't you cut down on the homework just a little? There's other things in life besides school, you know. Right, Gabe?"

Gabriel said nothing, but while he was watching her, Lucy found it almost impossible to concentrate.

After morning prayers Lucy heard laughter from across the room. A moment later all heads had turned toward the blackboard on the far wall. Lucy read what she'd written there and saw nothing to laugh at until she read the last line, an announcement that choir practice had been canceled. She'd spelled the word "quire."

The laughter and whispering drew Sister Andrew's attention. In a moment her shoulders were shaking with laughter under her black veil. The laughter in the room rose quickly to a roar that seemed to explode through Lucy's head. Sister Andrew's cheeks had turned bright pink; her eyes were sparkling with tears. Raising her voice above the noise, Sister Andrew said, "Lucy seems to have invented a new spelling."

Lucy turned her face toward the window. Without her noticing it, the geranium plants had grown full, round leaves. Where the sun shone through, their veins were a delicate, pale-green lace.

Someone close behind Lucy repeated Sister Andrew's joke: "The brain is inventing a new spelling." Lucy stood up without knowing why except that she had to do something. The sudden, complete silence made her hesitate; then she started up the aisle. She crossed the back of the room, then walked down the far aisle, scooping up an eraser from the blackboard ledge with one hand as she passed by. At the word *quire* she stopped and erased it with one fast, rough stroke. She wrote "choir" in huge letters, then threw the piece of chalk down. It hit the corner of the ledge and broke. Someone yelled, "Look out!" Hands and arms shot up for protection as sharp fragments of chalk flew in all directions. Raymond and some of the other boys sitting closest to the blackboard reached out to try to catch the pieces of chalk.

Gabriel hadn't moved at all, Lucy realized only after she'd returned to her desk, this time crossing the front of the room to show she didn't care that everyone was staring at her. But instead of sitting down, she went on to the back of the room and out the door. She stopped in the coatroom, unsure of what to do next, but when she heard Sister Andrew call her name, she took her coat from its hook and ran.

The twins glanced at Lucy when she came through the kitchen door, then went back to their toys, which lay scattered all around them on the floor. Paul-ette had seen nothing unusual in her coming home from school in the middle of the morning. But Mama looked up in shock from her ironing as Lucy rushed past her.

She threw open the door of Edward's room. Min Min had sneaked in somehow and lay asleep on the bed, a pool of black against the white bedspread. He jumped off and ran out, barely missing the door, which had bounced against the wall, then slammed shut again with a crash. Lucy dropped facedown on top of the bed. She'd run as fast as she could all the way home, and now that she'd stopped, her legs and her chest burned with pain. Her eyes were burning too, but they were still perfectly dry. At least she hadn't cried, she told herself—like Madeleine had.

The door opened with a quiet click. "Are you sick?" Mama asked.

"I'm not sick!" Lucy said angrily. "I'm just sick of school, and I'm *never* going back!" Then she pushed her face into the pillow.

"Has something happened? What's wrong?"

Lucy lifted her head, turned over onto her back, and took several deep breaths. "Nothing's wrong," she said calmly, and forced herself to smile. "It's too stupid to talk about." Mama came in and sat down at the foot of Edward's bed, but Lucy could tell that she was listening for sounds from the kitchen, where the twins were alone. "I'm never going back," Lucy repeated, quietly this time. "I'll get a job. I've had enough of school. More than enough, more than you and Papa ever had."

She closed her eyes. The bed shook, and when she opened her eyes Mama had left.

Lucy crawled underneath the white bedspread

and fell asleep. When she woke up, the hands of Edward's tiny clock were both pointing straight up. It was noon, and the class would just be letting out. She got up, washed her hands and face, and went downstairs. Mama had fixed grilled-cheese sandwiches and canned tomato soup. Lucy ate hungrily, and when Mama went upstairs to put away the ironing, Lucy stayed on at the table while Paul-ette finished their lunch. Mama had cut their cheese sandwiches into tiny squares, but instead of eating them, the twins had been lining them up one behind the other and pushing them around like toy trains. Paul was blowing air through his lips and making sputtering noises like a train engine.

Lucy still had a dull pain in her side from running, but the short sleep had made her see everything much more clearly. She could see, for one thing, that the twins always ate and played together as if they were one person. Right now, for example, Paul was taking half-chewed bites of sandwich from his own mouth and pushing them into Colette's mouth, which was wide open, like a baby bird's. In a minute Paul would be reaching inside his sister's mouth, taking the soggy bread out again, and putting it back in his own mouth.

She could also see perfectly clearly not only that she'd have to go back to school, but that she had to go back this afternoon. By tomorrow the story would be all over Saint Margaret's that she'd made a stupid mistake, then run out of class. But going back now would make it seem unimportant, as though she'd already forgotten.

Lucy looked at the kitchen clock. It was almost twelve thirty, and she'd missed recitation practice. But even here in the peaceful, cluttered kitchen, she could see and smell the perfect neatness of the convent music room. She could even feel the tension of standing before Mother Augusta, who was probably sitting on her piano bench at this very moment, wondering where she was.

Mama came back just as Lucy was lifting the twins down from their high chairs. "I'll be going now," Lucy said.

"Why don't you stay home and rest? It won't hurt you to miss a day. You can go back tomorrow."

"I have to go *now*."

Lucy arrived after the class had started reciting the rosary. No one seemed to notice her. The corrected announcement for choir practice was still on the blackboard. She sat down, closed her eyes, and repeated with the others, "Holy Mary, mother of God, pray for us sinners, now and at the hour of our death. Amen."

Lucy concentrated on the moment when the prayer would be over and people would open their eyes. They'd stare at her, and she wanted to act as though nothing had happened. She was still trying to decide whether to smile or look serious when her insides suddenly rose in a huge, sickening swelling. With her hands clamped tightly over her mouth, she ran out to the corridor and down the stairs. She had almost reached the steps to the basement when a tearing noise in her chest forced her to stop. She wrapped both arms around her waist and bent over. From her mouth poured all the food she'd eaten for lunch.

Dazed with horror, Lucy saw the puddle of lumpy, sour-smelling liquid spread, endlessly it seemed, along the floor at her feet. She sank to her knees. She heard noises close behind her and turned her head. The boys' stairs were crowded with people. The entire class seemed to have followed her and witnessed what she'd done. From nearby came the sound of knocking and Sister Andrew's calling, "Sister Rose, come quickly!" Then a darkness descended like a blanket and covered everything.

When Lucy regained consciousness, her arms were being tightly squeezed. Sister Andrew and Sister Rose were pulling her backward, one on each side, or trying to lift her up. They were hurting her arms, but when she tried to tell them to stop, the only sound she made was a moan, like an animal. She twisted her shoulders to free herself. She'd run away, and this time she'd die before she ever came near Saint Margaret's again. If only she could die right now.

"Return to your seats, please!" Sister Andrew's voice seemed far away. When Lucy tried to turn and make sure that the class was really leaving, the light of the corridor window cut across her vision. It looked like frost, or lace. The window disappeared, and she heard a sound deep inside her head, like a siren going off.

"Laurence, you can help us here." Sister Andrew's voice was very close. She hadn't taken the class away after all. Then Lucy felt herself being lifted. The movement made her insides churn sickeningly until Laurence had set her down on the couch in Sister Rose's office.

Sister Rose was smiling down at her. "You're going home in a taxi," she said, feeling Lucy's forehead.

"Let me stay home forever this time," Lucy prayed silently. "I'll never ask for anything again."

14

FOR THREE DAYS Lucy lay in the dimness of Edward's room. The dull, heavy pain had spread beyond the edges of her body and filled the space all around her. Light and sounds reached her only faintly, as if from another world. The time didn't pass one hour after the other, but seemed to open randomly at odd, unexpected places. On the first evening, Mama brought her a plate of dry toast and a cup of hot tea, which she left on the chair next to the bed. The toast smelled delicious and made Lucy very hungry. But she felt too weak to

166

reach for the plate and had to rest first. She closed her eyes for what she thought was a minute or two, and when she opened them again the room was dark. She felt around on the chair, but the cup and plate were gone. The next time she woke up, Jeanie was standing at the foot of the bed, dressed in her school clothes.

"What time is it?"

"About four thirty."

"In the afternoon?"

Jeanie laughed. "Of course! Mama wants to know if you need anything."

Lucy tried, but she couldn't think. "No," she said finally.

"Are you better?"

"Yes," Lucy said, wishing Jeanie would leave. Jeanie had just come home from school, and she didn't want to hear her say anything that had to do with Saint Margaret's.

"It's so dark in here," Jeanie said. "Shall I light the candle?"

"I don't care."

After lighting the candle, Jeanie slid the statue forward so that its face looked down into the flame; then she left, closing the door behind her. Lucy's eyes were drawn to the statue's brightly illuminated face, which seemed alive above the dancing flame of the candle. On the wall behind it the statue's veiled head threw a half circle of moving shadow.

When Lucy closed her eyes, she could still see the candle flame inside the red glass. She'd just been dreaming about lighted candles, she suddenly realized, only these had been several feet tall and cream colored. They had stood on the floor, one at each corner of her bed, exactly like the candles that had stood at the corners of Papa's coffin. There'd been flowers all around her too, like those that had surrounded Papa, white lilies, roses, and carnations, some massed like snowbanks and others in fan-shaped bouquets in elegant baskets with high, round handles. In the dream she'd been dead, like Papa and Victor, but instead of feeling sad or terrified, she'd felt at peace and content.

The following day Jeanie offered to get Lucy some books from the Rockford Public Library, but she refused. She couldn't stand the thought of reading, or even of just holding a book. She spent most of her waking hours looking around Edward's room. The pattern of wallpaper border along the top edge of the walls reminded Lucy of a plumed helmet, as though knights in armor were standing guard outside the wall, with only their heads visible. Their elegant helmets were completely unlike the plain round one that had hung from Victor's pack. The first time Jeanie saw it, she had mistaken it for a cooking pot. Everyone had laughed, but Victor explained that it could be used in an emergency to heat food over an open fire. He said he hoped to try it someday. Lucy wondered if Victor had ever had a chance to use his helmet for cooking, and how the meal had turned out.

She'd seen hundreds of soldiers marching through Rockford and in newsreels at the movies. Like the perfect row of knights in the wallpaper border, each soldier had moved exactly like the rest. But real soldiers were of different heights, and each wore his helmet at a slightly different angle.

When Lucy was well enough to go downstairs, she had to stay on the sofa, covered with blankets. On Saturday afternoon Edward raked the yard, and from the living-room window she watched him scrape the dead leaves and debris across the sidewalk and into a pile next to the street. There was to be a bonfire after supper.

"Why don't you come out?" Edward asked Lucy. "Or do you intend to stay indoors for the rest of your life?"

Lucy stayed at the window and watched Edward let Jeanie strike the matches and start the fire. Each time the front door opened, the smell of burning leaves floated indoors. The fire had drawn all the children in the neighborhood, and as darkness fell their shadows and red, glowing faces were like the pictures Lucy had seen in geography books of people who worked and lived around open fires. She'd always been so sure that she'd travel to such places. But now, just as Edward said, she didn't think she could leave the house ever again.

Alice came almost every day, and one day Mama took advantage of her visit to fit a costume she'd been sewing for Alice's dance recital in June.

"My mother's had another one of her big ideas," Alice said. "It's supposed to be a surprise again but I'll tell you anyway, Lucy, because it's very funny. I'm doing a tap dance with another girl, only we'll both be dressed like men in black tuxedos and top hats. We'll have our hair tucked up inside the hats."

"That is funny," Lucy said, though all she could manage was a weak smile.

"The funniest part will come at the very end, when we take off our hats and let our hair fall down." Alice moved her hands upward from her head as if lifting off an invisible hat.

170

Lucy looked at Alice's hair, which was still curly and not much longer than it had been for the Ice Carnival. "But your hair won't fall, will it?"

"Yes it will. I'm having it straightened."

"I didn't know you could have hair straightened," Lucy said.

"Sure you can." Alice laughed. "You can do just about anything with your looks nowadays."

After she'd gone, Edward said, "Alice's hair will fall out if she doesn't stop messing with it."

"It won't," Lucy said. Edward's remark had caused an image to flash into Lucy's mind, of Alice triumphantly removing her top hat at the end of the dance and uncovering, before the horrified audience, a head that was completely bald.

When Lucy went back to school, she'd been absent only a little more than a week, though it had seemed like a year.

After morning recess she went up to the nuns' study as usual. It was the only place in school where she felt she belonged. Although the exams were less than two weeks away, she spent most of the hour standing on a chair, looking out the high window. In the short time she'd been gone, the hills had become dense mounds in every shade of green.

When the noon bell finally rang, Lucy paused on her way out to look at the *Angelus* picture.

171

Knowing that it contained no message about Gabriel made her feel empty and light. She'd wanted Gabriel to think she was different from other girls, and he probably *did* think that, now that he'd seen her throw up in front of the whole class.

Lucy walked to Saint Margaret's Church after class and sat listening to the pounding and shouting in the church basement. When she went back to the classroom, she found Sister Andrew alone at her desk. Her hands were folded in her lap and she was staring at the pink-and-gold clouds and bright-blue sky outside the window. It was the first time Lucy had ever seen Sister Andrew doing nothing. She sat down at her own desk.

Sister Andrew turned and said quietly, "I was glad to see you back in class today. You seem prepared to continue your studies for the competition, though Sister Rose tells me that you are probably not well enough. Since the regional examinations are taking place here at Saint Margaret's, it would be a courtesy if you were to take them with the other candidates. However, you must prepare for disappointment."

Although Sister Andrew had spoken softly, even kindly, Lucy felt the old, dull anger rise. "I don't have to *prepare*," she said. "I've been ready all along. Haven't I said from the start that I didn't stand a chance of winning?"

"You *said* you had no chance of winning," Sister Andrew said, "but you may have been trying to protect yourself by refusing to make the attempt in the first place. In my judgment that would have been the only true failure."

Lucy's mouth opened, then closed. The brilliant colors were gone from the sky, and the room was growing dark. After a silence Sister Andrew said, "I realize now that I did you an injustice by persuading you to enter the competition. I was sure that it would help you discover your own powers and encourage you to cultivate them."

"I already know—"

"I understand how you feel."

"People always say that," Lucy interrupted. "Nobody knows how I feel," she shouted. "Nobody cares, either, as long as I do what *they* want."

When Lucy stopped shouting, Sister Andrew said calmly, "Do you know why I'm here at Saint Margaret's?"

Lucy was too confused to talk or listen to anything more. She wanted only to run home, fall onto Edward's bed, and go to sleep. "I know you're really Doctor something," she said wearily, "and that you write books. A lot of people are wondering why someone like that would have come to teach in Rockford."

"I am here because wiser persons realized that

the tasks we do least willingly are the most worthy in the sight of God," Sister Andrew said, then reached inside her desk and brought out some papers. Lucy recognized her own handwriting and saw that it was covered, as usual, with Sister Andrew's markings.

In the days that followed, Sister Andrew asked Lucy often if she felt strong enough to work. Lucy always chose to stay and went home even later than before. Sometimes she waited for Sister Andrew so that they could walk out together.

During her absence Sister Andrew and Mother Augusta had decided to change her recitation poem. The new poem was about Saint Francis of Assisi preaching to the birds. It was cheerful, and much shorter.

Now that she had no chance of placing first and going to a movie with Gabriel, Lucy had stopped worrying about the judges and actually looked forward to discussing her work with Sister Andrew. She began to wish that the exams would never come and that this separate routine, which she'd found so lonely in the beginning, might continue until the last day of school in June, when she'd be leaving Saint Margaret's forever.

15

On FRIDAY MORNING Lucy overslept and was almost late arriving at the church basement for the first regional exam, essay writing. All the other candidates were sitting at a long table with a young priest. Though they were all strangers to Lucy, they were busily conversing as if they'd known each other for a long time.

Only one person looked at Lucy as she came in—a short, fat boy with damp comb marks in his hair. The only empty chair remaining was next to him. As soon as Lucy had sat down in it, he said, "I hope you're not superstitious." At Lucy's

175

puzzled look, he pointed to a card in front of her. "You're number thirteen."

The boy's hands were dimpled across the knuckles, like a baby's. He seemed much too young to be in the eighth grade. Lucy was about to ask his age, just to be talking like everyone else. But before she could speak, the boy said, "My name is Scott Lalande," and went on to explain that he'd been adopted by a family who were very poor and already had many children. "I want to repay their kindness to me by winning a scholarship."

Lucy listened in amazement.

"Your school sent only one candidate," he went on, after waiting for her to speak. "All the rest of us are in pairs, a boy and a girl."

His sentences came in a dizzying rush, and when he stopped to catch his breath, Lucy recognized the thin whistling of asthma in his throat. Papa's asthma had often sounded like that, as though he had to push and pull the air through his lungs. Since her fall on Alice's rink, she knew how that felt.

All conversation stopped while the priest walked around the table and placed sheets of lined paper and two long, newly sharpened pencils in front of each candidate. "You have two hours," he announced. "When I raise my hand, you may begin."

At the signal, Lucy turned the papers over and read the instructions. "Write a composition on the following subject: Describe what you would buy if someone gave you one hundred dollars."

Scott immediately started to write. Lucy glanced around the table. Most of the other candidates had also started, and their rapidly moving pencils reminded her of Sister Andrew's warning, "Don't write the first thing that comes into your mind."

But after several minutes nothing at all had come into Lucy's mind. What *would* she do with so much money? A hundred dollars was enough to buy all the candy and treats she'd ever wanted, but she couldn't write for two hours about candy. For one thing, the judges would think it showed greediness. They wouldn't be interested or impressed, no matter how well she described how hard it was to share each bar of chocolate with Jeanie and Edward. For weeks the stores had been selling Easter candy, and with a hundred dollars she could buy plenty for everybody. She'd buy herself what she'd always wanted, a giant chocolate egg beautifully decorated with sugar flowers, and have it all to herself. She'd buy Jeanie an elegant Easter basket filled with chocolate and candy arranged on a bed of green paper straw.

Lucy could almost taste the chocolate, but the

paper in front of her was still blank. She kept her eyes down, but at the edge of her vision she had already seen the flash of pages being turned. Others had already filled one page and started the second. She couldn't tell whether five minutes or half an hour had gone by. She looked at the wall above the priest's head, where a clock would be in a classroom, but instead met the priest's worried eyes.

She gripped the pencil tightly and set the point down on the top corner of the page. If she had a hundred dollars, she'd buy gifts for everybody— for Mama, the twins, Claire and Alice. She'd even buy something for Sister Andrew. But what could she buy for a nun? And if she was buying gifts for so many people, she could give something to Gabriel too, like a book.

Books were much better gifts to write about than candy. The idea wasn't interesting or original, but after all she was only taking these exams out of politeness to the other candidates. All she had to do was write something. Other people were probably also writing about using the money to buy gifts for their families and friends and teachers. Everyone here would know what she knew, that the judges would approve of such unselfishness. In fact, it was probably what she *would* do, except that she'd buy something for herself too. She must be sure to put that in.

Lucy quickly wrote down a list of names including Alice and Claire. Next to Claire's name she wrote "dentist." She'd pay the dentist so that Claire wouldn't have to wait to have her teeth fixed for free. But the directions said to write about "buying' something, and it was important to follow the directions exactly. Sister Andrew had warned her about that too. And wouldn't paying the dentist be like reminding Claire that her teeth needed fixing?

Lucy stopped writing.

"Do you need something?" the priest whispered from behind her chair. He had walked over without making a sound.

"I was just thinking," Lucy whispered back, and began to write.

Writing about gifts was too complicated, she decided, thinking fast. She'd use all the money to buy books. How many books? A lot of cheap ones, or just a few expensive books covered with leather? She made some quick notes, then paused. Why buy books when the library was filled with more books than one person would ever want or be able to read? But in the Rockford Public Library there were almost no French books. She'd buy French books, and after reading them she'd donate them to the library.

Or maybe she'd buy one expensive book, not to read and then keep on a shelf, but a thick book with plenty of interesting pictures. She'd spent hours looking at such books in the library because no one was allowed to take them home. One book she'd looked at most often contained pictures of pages from ancient religious books. Each page was handwritten and decorated with fine drawings of flowers or animals or scenes from the Bible in colors that glowed, like tiny stained-glass windows. The decorated letters were fine and intricate, and she'd enjoyed figuring out what they were. A dragon with a long curved tail had turned out to be a G.

Lucy made short notes of these ideas, in single words or phrases. Sister Andrew had taught the whole class to do this, but she'd made Lucy practice the method until she'd learned to write complete essays in a very short time on much harder subjects than this one.

Until the eighth grade, Lucy had always written the usual way. Ideas and the words for them had come easily, not like today, and she'd always finished before anybody else. She hadn't tried very hard to change the way she wrote until after the Shrove Tuesday party and Gabriel's invitation. It made no difference now, but at least it was helping her make up for the time she'd already lost, and she'd have a paper to hand in like the others.

She'd arranged her notes in groups, as Sister Andrew had taught her, and once the page was filled she knew she had more than she needed. She quickly chose the biggest group, a list of details describing one illustrated page that was completely different from the rest. She'd describe that, she decided, and say that if she had a hundred dollars she'd buy the book it had come from.

The page she'd chosen to write about was less colorful than any of the others and probably not as old, but it was the one she remembered best. Besides, the pictures were simpler and easier to describe in detail in the short time she had left. The writing on the page was framed with tiny drawings of monks in brown robes. Their faces were turned toward the center, as if they were reading what was written inside the frame. Their hands were together in prayer, not tightly but touching only at the fingertips. The halo behind each monk's head was a flat golden disk.

One day, after Lucy had been examining the pictures for a long time, she had seen the librarian coming toward her. She'd expected to be reprimanded, probably for looking at the book so long, but the librarian had brought her a magnifying glass that allowed Lucy to see that each halo had a fine lacy pattern in darker gold, and that no two monks were exactly alike. Even their feet were different. All wore sandals, but some were partly hidden under the folds of the robes. Some of the kneeling monks had their long toes curled forward, as if they were tired and ready to lean backward against their heels.

Lucy had just started to write her essay when the priest announced that one hour had passed. "By now you should have your rough copy almost finished," he said. Lucy knew she wouldn't have time to write more than one copy. That meant she'd have to work not only fast, but neatly as well.

She wrote without stopping, and by the time the priest had announced that they had twenty minutes left she was almost through. Her plan had worked, but she still needed an interesting way to end her essay. Several people had already finished recopying. They were reading their final papers and making small corrections. Lucy reread hers.

She was pleased with what she'd written, but when she'd read it through, she still hadn't thought of a closing. Her fingers were cramped and the pencil was slippery with sweat. Her hand started to shake. She needed to stand up and walk around, as she'd always done in the nuns' study whenever she was tired or stuck. But none of the others had moved from their chairs except the priest.

Lucy glanced again through what she'd written. The essay stopped, as if its last page had gotten lost, but she couldn't think of anything more to say. In desperation she wrote that the picture in the ancient book itself would be even more beautiful than the one in the library, especially since the halos would be drawn in real gold leaf. This didn't seem like enough. She added, quoting from the introduction to the library book, that such rare, ancient books needed special care and had to be kept in sealed cases, away from light and air, and that only scholars were permitted to study them.

The table was almost empty, with only Lucy and two other girls left. She could hear the other candidates talking excitedly just outside the door to the church basement. A burst of laughter made the words in front of Lucy seem to melt together. A mere hundred dollars would not be enough! Such a rare and ancient book would be priceless, and what she'd written was ridiculous. It would make the judges laugh.

The two girls had handed in their papers and

were chatting in low voices with the priest. If she left now, with her papers, the priest wouldn't notice. As if he'd read her thoughts, the priest looked down the table at Lucy.

She erased the last few lines and started to write, her pencil moving rapidly, almost by itself. Because such books were so rare and precious, she wrote, she'd buy only one page, the one with the little monks if possible, and have it framed under glass for protection. If even one page cost more than a hundred dollars, she added frantically, she'd buy her own copy of the library book—and a magnifying glass.

While she was still writing, the priest said, "Lucy Delaroche." He'd raised his voice, since they were the only two people left in the room. "It's ten minutes past twelve. Please hand in your papers." Feeling his eyes upon her, Lucy quickly arranged the pages in order, wrote her number, 13, at the top of each one, and placed them on his outstretched hands.

All the other candidates had left by the time Lucy started her walk home through the cemetery. After the cool dimness of the church basement the bright, half-grown leaves and the dappled sunlight were blinding. If she'd written her essay the old way, she might have been part of the cheerful, laughing crowd outside the door of the church basement instead of the very last to finish. The judges would probably joke among themselves about how unlucky the number thirteen had turned out to be. And when the results were announced tomorrow night, everyone would know that the candidate from Saint Margaret's, in spite of working past the stopping time, had written the worst essay.

Lucy had the number 13 for all the exams, and was the last to recite that afternoon. Some of the candidates talked among themselves while they waited their turn, but Lucy couldn't stop thinking of the morning.

When her turn came to recite, Lucy was surprised to see Mother Augusta among the judges. "This is Lucy Delaroche, a pupil at Saint Margaret's," Mother Augusta said proudly, and Lucy felt sorry for her.

To her own surprise, Lucy's recitation was the best she'd ever given. Her sense of hopelessness made her relax, so her voice was steady and her gestures natural. "Be sure to look at the judges," Mother Augusta had reminded her at the end of their final practice session. Lucy had been sure she'd be too nervous, but she found it much easier to look at a group of strangers than at Mother Augusta alone, sitting on her piano bench.

185

It was four thirty by the time Lucy finished. Although she was tired and wanted most of all to go home, she decided to tell Sister Andrew right away about the essay. Sister Andrew was alone, working at her desk. When Lucy entered the room, she looked up expectantly. Lucy stopped next to her own desk and looked down for a moment at the school yard, which was deserted. Today had been the last day of school before Easter vacation.

"It's a wonder these plants didn't die over the winter," Lucy said, touching the soft, new geranium leaves. It didn't seem fair, now that she was here, to disappoint Sister Andrew by telling her about the essay. "The recitation went better than I thought it would," Lucy said. The leaf she'd been holding broke off in her fingers. Sister Andrew said nothing. "The writing this morning didn't go very well," she said quickly with a tight, nervous laugh. "I had a hard time getting started, and then I had a hard time finishing. I made a mistake choosing what to write about."

Lucy turned her back to the window. The classroom was bright with daylight, but it felt as tense and suffocating at this moment as on that dark winter afternoon when she'd tried so hard to stay out of the competiton. Sister Andrew was waiting now, with exactly the same calm and silence, for her to explain.

"What subject were you given for the essay?" Sister Andrew asked. When Lucy had told her, she said only, "I see."

"I know it should have been easy," Lucy said, "but I found it hard, almost impossible." She rushed on, hoping to keep Sister Andrew from asking what she'd written about. "Nobody else seemed to find it hard. I was the only one. I didn't prepare myself well enough," she said, remembering the hours she'd wasted in the nuns' study, feeling trapped and thinking about Gabriel.

"On the contrary, it seems more likely that you were overprepared for such a simple subject." Sister Andrew took off her glasses and rubbed her eyes with her handkerchief. She looked sad and very tired.

Sister Andrew, Lucy realized for the first time, must have received only respect and admiration for her work. Now, because she was the one who had prepared Lucy for these exams, she'd probably be criticized, exactly as if she herself had failed. She might even be laughed at. Not even Laurence Constantine had ever failed as miserably as Lucy had today. And Laurence had never pretended to be something he wasn't.

16

WHEN LUCY GOT HOME from the Saturday exam on French Literature, she found the house unusually quiet. All the chores had been done, including hers, and the twins were asleep. Jeanie was also asleep. The dining-room door was closed, and on its knob, pinned to a hanger, hung the Saint Bernadette costume: a plain gray novice's dress the convent had sent over and that Mama had cut down to fit Jeanie, a white apron and head scarf made from an old bedsheet, and a pair of Tessa's long black convent stockings.

Mama was in the living room hemming the

velvet dress she'd made for Lucy to wear to the announcements. The wine-colored material had come from a woman Mama sewed for regularly. It had a flaw, a pale line down the center. To avoid it, Mama had cut Lucy's dress in long panels, narrow at the top and widening from the waist into a skirt that fell in soft, deep folds at the hem, like the petals of a flower. The dress also had long, narrow sleeves. They were so narrow and tight, in fact, that Lucy hadn't been able to get her hands through them at first. Mama had cut some openings at the wrists, then spent hours making the round, velvet-covered buttons and velvet loops to close them.

Because the color was dark for spring, Mama had crocheted a white lace collar and matching cuffs.

"Don't you think the white is too Christmassy-looking?" Tessa commented. The next day Tessa came home from work very excited because one of the customers at the beauty shop had suggested dyeing the lace with strong tea. The tea had turned the collar and cuffs a very pale brown, like antique lace, so now the dress looked even more elegant and old-fashioned than before.

There'd been no way Lucy could stop their preparations. She couldn't tell them the truth, that it would only make everything worse to have to stand there, more dressed up than she'd ever been in her life and probably more than any of the other girls would be, and watch others receive the prizes. All she could do was hope nobody from her class would be there, at least not Gabriel or Madeleine.

Lucy took a bath and washed her hair. While she was sitting on the back porch drying it in the sun, Tessa came home from work with a curling iron. "The manager at the beauty shop let me borrow it to fix your hair for tonight," Tessa said. She ran her fingers through Lucy's damp hair. "Come inside, before it's completely dry." After brushing Lucy's hair smooth, Tessa turned the ends under with the curling iron. "Everybody at the shop wishes you luck," she said. Lucy kept her head down and didn't answer. When Tessa held the mirror up, Lucy didn't recognize herself. She looked almost pretty, she thought.

Edward stopped to watch. "I won't be ashamed to have people know you're my sister," he teased. You will be, Lucy thought. Jeanie and the twins were up, and everybody was laughing and talking excitedly. Only Lucy was quiet. She felt old and miserable and very wise, like the person in a story who knows before anybody else that something bad is about to happen.

*　　*　　*

The church basement was brightly lit, and the floor was covered with chairs arranged in straight rows facing the stage. Lucy entered with the other candidates and sat in the first row, which was marked RESERVED with a long strip of pale-blue paper.

The girls had all looked very ordinary only a few hours earlier, when taking the exams. Some had worn clothes even more dull and plain than Lucy's. But tonight they were transformed in new-looking pastel dresses. The girl sitting next to Lucy, whose dress was light purple, was also wearing a small bunch of silk lilacs in her hair. The flowers made the girl's plain brown hair look very pretty, and Lucy wished she'd accepted Tessa's offer of an ornamental comb for her own hair.

Even the boys looked different in their suits and ties. Scott looked older in his dark jacket, and not nearly so fat.

The parish hall filled up quickly. People were standing at the back and in the aisles by the time Mr. Godin, the school inspector, walked onto the stage. "The first item on our program this evening is a presentation of *The Life of Saint Bernadette*, by the students of Saint Margaret's School. The results of the annual regional scholarship competition and the awarding of prizes will follow immediately."

Jeanie's first entrance as Bernadette was from the far right, a part of the stage that Lucy couldn't see. At first she only heard Jeanie's voice, but when Jeanie moved to the center of the stage, Lucy hardly recognized her. She looked much taller in the gray dress and white apron, which reached almost to her ankles. She had on lipstick and rouge, and her head scarf had been tied in a loose knot under her hair, exactly like the picture of *The Gleaners* in the nuns' study.

At the other end of the stage, which Lucy could see clearly, a grotto had been built out of gray canvas draped and painted to look like rocks. Branches from real trees had been brought in, to make the rocks look more real, but their new green leaves were dying under the hot lights. Someone appeared offstage and stood among the shadows for a moment before stepping through the grotto and into the light. It was Madeleine, dressed as the Virgin in a long white robe and a blue veil. A lamp had gone on behind her to give the effect of a heavenly vision suddenly appearing. The dazzling spotlight shone directly into Lucy's eyes, so that Madeleine seemed miraculously afloat.

The second act opened with loud shouting and

the noise of scuffling, pounding feet. Lucy recognized for the first time the sounds she'd been hearing while she sat in church after school. In this act, Bernadette's father was shouting and threatening to beat her for telling lies about seeing the Virgin. Lucy couldn't see at first who was playing the part of Jeanie's father. It wasn't until he and Jeanie had moved to the center of the stage that she saw it was Gabriel. He was pulling Jeanie roughly across the stage with one hand, with his other hand raised high, as if ready to slap her.

Lucy had been perched tensely on the edge of her chair, trying to see. She collapsed back into her seat, dazed with disbelief. Raymond appeared next, dressed as a policeman. Someone had borrowed a real uniform, and Lucy was shocked that so much work and preparation could have gone on without her knowing, as if she'd been in another country while it was happening. The policeman had come to arrest Saint Bernadette, but her father now believed in the vision and tried to stop him. When Lucy saw Gabriel wrap his arms tightly around Jeanie to protect her from Raymond, she had to look away.

At the end of the play the curtains closed, then opened again. Jeanie, who had been lying dead in the last scene, now stood between Madeleine and Gabriel. They held hands as they smiled and bowed, Gabriel holding in his free hand the white lily he'd placed on Jeanie's chest in the last scene. Jeanie, dressed as a nun, had lain perfectly still, as if she really had died, while Gabriel carefully set the flower on her folded hands.

The applause reminded Lucy that the exam announcements were about to begin. She was proud of Jeanie, but she knew she could never forgive her not mentioning that Gabriel was also in the play. Jeanie, who always told Lucy everything down to the smallest details, had kept secret the one thing Lucy would have wanted to know. And Lucy had sat for hours like a fool, all by herself in the empty church, without ever suspecting that the noises she heard were the play rehearsals and that very close by was a better chance than she'd ever hoped for to see Gabriel and talk with him.

The curtain opened again, this time on a half circle of chairs. Lucy followed the other candidates up the steps to the stage and sat down. On one side stood a table with neat stacks of books tied in bundles with white ribbons. The audience was a blur of faces in the darkness beyond the lights. Mr. Godin made a speech, and while he was talking Lucy saw the people who had been in the play creep in two or three at a time and sit in the empty chairs of the front row. Gabriel took the chair in the middle, between Raymond and

194

Madeleine. Jeanie came in last, when there were no chairs left and people were sitting on the floor. Lucy saw Gabriel wave to Jeanie, then point at the empty space in front of his chair. Jeanie hurried over and sat down with her back resting against Gabriel's legs. Gabriel placed both his hands on her shoulders. They looked like a real father and daughter.

Mr. Godin was introducing the candidates. Lucy didn't hear her own name and had to stand up quickly after the girl in the purple dress pushed her elbow. She started to sit down again right away, but Mr. Godin signaled that she was to remain standing. Lucy's dress was uncomfortably hot as she stood waiting for Mr. Godin to finish explaining to the audience that Saint Bernadette and the candidate for Saint Margaret's were sisters. Lucy sat down to laughter and applause, followed by a single long, piercing whistle. She tried to see if Edward had whistled so loudly, but she was too embarrassed from being singled out to look beyond the blinding stage lights.

Far at the back, beyond the expanse of clapping hands, Lucy noticed for the first time the row of quiet, veiled figures. Seeing the nuns, and especially the thought that Sister Andrew must be sitting among them, made her wish even more desperately that the announcements were over.

But Mr. Godin seemed ready to make them last as long as possible. A movement in the front row made Lucy look down. Gabriel and Raymond were leaning toward each other in front of Madeleine, and Raymond was whispering excitedly.

Lucy had to force her attention back to Mr. Godin, who was explaining the rules of the competition. "There are three prizes, first, second and third, in each of the four categories. Two overall winners, a boy and girl, will travel to Ottawa in two weeks' time and take the final examinations, which will determine the winner of the final prize, a four-year scholarship."

It seemed so long ago that she'd struggled with her terrible essay, yet it was only yesterday morning, and in this very room. The third prizes had been awarded. Before long the announcements would be over and no one would remember that she'd sat here, dressed up in lace and velvet, like a princess almost, without winning even one third prize. It didn't matter that Gabriel was there, only a few feet away, because he wasn't paying attention. He was busy whispering with Raymond and Madeleine, and all Lucy could see was the top of his head.

Lucy heard her name called. She'd placed second in recitation, her worst subject. It felt so much like a miracle to have won something that by the time she was back in her chair with her prize of books resting in her lap, she was faint with joy. A few moments later she heard her name again. Mr. Godin was announcing the first prizes now, and he added that Lucy had written a perfect exam in French grammar. She'd forgotten how easy the grammar questions had seemed compared to the ones Sister Andrew had asked her. Before Lucy could get back to her chair, she heard her name again, this time as winner of the first prize in French literature. That exam had also seemed so much easier than she'd expected that she'd been sure afterward that she'd misunderstood the questions.

There was long applause, then silence. After waiting for Lucy to sit down, Mr. Godin announced that she'd won first prize for French composition, and laughed when his words were drowned out by the explosion of clapping and cheering. Lucy had been trying to balance her three prizes on her knees and had to be prodded again by the girl who had pushed her elbow the first time. This brought on a roar of laughter and more applause. Some people had stood up, and Lucy saw Edward among them with his hands clasped tightly above his head, like a prizefighter.

Lucy stood up. One of the ribbons had come undone, and as the books slid out of her grasp,

Jeanie's glasses flashed at the edge of the stage. "Lucy!" Jeanie yelled, her arms reaching into the light for Lucy's prizes. Lucy had to kneel to hand the books down to Jeanie. When she stood up again, she brushed her skirt where it had touched the floor, and as she did so she noticed that Jeanie had sat down in the empty chair between Raymond and Madeleine.

". . . special mention of the originality and remarkable maturity of thought and expression," Mr. Godin was saying. After accepting her prize and returning to her seat, Lucy looked again at the first row. Gabriel wasn't there. She looked at the row of nuns, but she still couldn't tell if Sister Andrew was among them. When Mr. Godin announced that Lucy had placed first in the regional competition, her mind couldn't absorb the meaning of his words. All she could think of was that Gabriel had been chatting with Raymond and Madeleine through most of the awarding of prizes, and that he hadn't been interested enough to stay until the end to see who won.

Scott had placed second, first among the boys, and would go to the finals too. Lucy had to stand next to him while someone took a picture of them holding framed metal plaques, the top awards. Then a crowd of people pushed forward to congratulate them.

Mother Augusta took out her handkerchief and touched the corners of her eyes with it after giving Lucy a quick, dignified hug. Sister Andrew held Lucy's hand, then looked at Lucy for a long time as if she wanted to say something.

"Do you want me to . . ." Lucy asked, although the thought that she might now have to go to school during Easter vacation cast a shadow over her sense of victory and triumph.

"No." Sister Andrew laughed. "What will help you most will be to have a good rest before taking the finals."

Lucy didn't see Claire until most of the crowd had drifted outside. But seeing her made it seem true for the first time that she had actually won. She was filled with sudden overflowing happiness that made her rush forward and throw her arms around Claire. "I'm so glad you came," she said.

"Didn't I tell you this would happen?" Claire said. "I'm so proud! I guess this means you'll be going out with Gabriel." Claire's words were thick and blurred, as if she'd started lisping, and when she saw that Lucy had noticed, her mouth opened in a quick, shy smile. Where Claire's front teeth had been, there was only blackness.

Claire laughed. "You should see your face! But don't worry, it's not as bad as it looks. The dentist said my teeth were too far gone to save, so he's making me some nice new ones. What did Gabriel say when he found out you'd won?"

"I don't think he even knows," Lucy stammered. "Anyway, he's probably forgotten by now. Shrove Tuesday was a long time ago, and so much has happened since then."

"You'll hear from him," Claire said confidently. "Maybe he didn't want to talk to you about it with so many people around."

Outside, Lucy found Mama and the rest of the family waiting for her. Other people were still standing around talking and laughing, and even in the dark Lucy could tell that Gabriel wasn't among them.

By the time she woke up the next morning, Lucy was sure that Claire must be right and that she'd hear from Gabriel, maybe today. She'd see him every day in church during the coming week, Holy Week. He might speak to her there, or he might telephone. He might even call her today. If he did, and if he asked her to a movie as soon as Lent was over next Saturday, she'd have a whole week to look forward to it.

While Lucy was eating breakfast, Jeanie came in carrying her collection of Easter candy, on which she'd spent most of the money Tessa gave her for taking care of the twins. She'd bought chocolate eggs, bunnies, and chicks, most of them from the dime store. They were made of soft, hollow chocolate, and Jeanie's constant handling had worn away the fine details of eyes and feathers, and some of the pieces were already chipped or broken.

"If I lick my fingers instead of washing them and they taste of chocolate, will it count as eating candy during Lent?" Jeanie asked. Lucy was finding the candy very tempting, and resisting the sweet smell added to her tension each time she heard the telephone. It had been ringing all morning with calls of congratulations, some from people she didn't know, but no call had come from Gabriel.

"Better wash your hands," she told Jeanie. "Lent will be over in only one more week."

"Less than a week," Jeanie corrected. "Lent will be over six days from now."

Six days, Lucy repeated silently. In six days at this hour she might be sitting next to Gabriel in the warm, popcorn-smelling dark of the Arcadian Theatre.

Lucy stayed on at the table, watching Jeanie.

"Are you surprised that you won?" Jeanie asked.

"Yes. I still can't believe it," Lucy said. "The

play was a surprise too," she added, hoping to make Jeanie start talking about Gabriel. She was afraid to do it herself.

"It was *supposed* to be a surprise! Mother Augusta *told* us not to talk about it. She said it would make announcement night more special. It was, wasn't it?"

Did Gabriel ever mention me? Lucy wanted to ask. Did he know you're my sister? Did he ever say anything to you about a little ring in a blue box?

Jeanie was arranging her chocolate animals on paper straw in a battered Easter basket that had once belonged to Lucy. She left, and Lucy sat alone in the silent kitchen. There was nothing to do and nothing she wanted to do, and yet she felt ready to explode.

After all the loneliness, the hopes, the humiliations of the past weeks, and especially after the surprise and excitement of winning, Lucy couldn't sit still. She felt like taking another long Sunday walk, something she hadn't done since before her illness. If Gabriel called while she was gone, he'd know she wasn't just staying home, waiting. Besides, she'd probably hear from him when she wasn't expecting to.

At the bottom of the porch steps Lucy turned to the right. The rocks sparkled in the sun, and their reflected heat made her want to skip and run, but she had to place her feet carefully among them on the narrow path. She stopped often to rest and to look up at the sky. She'd never seen it so blue and so deep, or the clouds so white.

After Mass that morning, perfect strangers had spoken to her on the steps of the church. Gabriel's parents might ask him about the girl who had won the competition. They might be asking him at this very moment.

She'd walk all the way to the lake, Lucy decided, since it was such an unusually beautiful day. The longer she was gone from home, the better chance there was that Gabriel would have telephoned when she got back.

Every crack in the rocks was bulging with thick brown and green moss, like tiny forests. When she climbed over a high rock, the wind caught her hair and lifted it. It was still smooth against her face from Tessa's brushing. From now on she'd follow the advice given in Alice's magazines and brush her hair every day instead of just combing it. By the summer it would be long enough to braid or pin up in hot, humid weather. And after this year she'd never again have to put on Tessa's old convent tunic, again. All the girls at Rockford High wore brightly-colored, pleated skirts and short white socks, which were never allowed at Saint Margaret's School, even on the very hot days.

Lucy imagined herself walking with Gabriel after school through the golden September sunshine. On weekends they might walk together in the woods through the brown, gold, red autumn leaves and later on through the gray lacy shadows of the bare branches.

Lucy had reached the edge of the cliff. Far below, the lake was a rich, deep green, its water rising in long slow waves with moving shafts of paler green where the sun's rays shone through. Along the base of the curved wall bright threads of light reflected off the glittering water and wove back and forth over the smooth surface of the rock.

Only a few weeks ago she had stood where she was standing now and imagined herself drowning and freezing to death. And today, maybe at this very moment, someone at home might be answering the telephone, "I'm sorry, she isn't here. Would you like to leave a message?" At this very moment Gabriel's voice might be coming into her house.

Although the thought made Lucy want to run back right away, she sat down. She had to pull her knees up and hold them tightly inside her arms, because with so much space all around, and with the wind blowing so freely across the lake and over the flat landscape, she felt like one of those winged seeds from maple trees, ready to float away on the air.

In two weeks she actually would be traveling to Ottawa to take the final exams. That trip would be just the beginning of all the traveling she planned to do in the future. And after last night her life at school would never be the same. Everybody would want to be her friend, and every day would be like the time she came out of school after the Shrove Tuesday party. It would be better, in fact, now that she'd actually accomplished what had seemed impossible to her back then.

Lucy stayed until the sun was close to the horizon on the opposite side of the lake. Although the landscape looked flatter and more gentle in the slanting light, the walk back proved much more difficult. The twisted path was now full of dark shadows between the rocks, so Lucy kept misjudging and losing her footing. Her legs were stiff and sore, too, from being curled up for so long, and when they collapsed suddenly from under her, she scraped her hands and knees against the rough surface of the rocks.

When Lucy got home, there was a message that Alice had come by, very excited, and wanted to know when Lucy's picture would appear in the

Rockford *Times*. There was no word from Gabriel, but there was still plenty of time.

The following week, Holy Week, Lucy went to church every day. She watched Gabriel assisting the priest at the services. He seemed wonderfully grown-up and serious in his starched white robe as he knelt and rose, moving soundlessly on the carpeted steps in front of the altar. On Holy Thursday, as usual, Father Martin washed the feet of twelve first- and second-grade boys representing the Apostles. Gabriel held the basin while the priest poured a small amount of water over each little boy's foot. Several of the boys giggled or tried to move their feet away from the stream of water, which must have been cold, or the towel, which must have tickled. Father Martin didn't smile when that happened, nor did Gabriel, in spite of the fact that everyone in Saint Margaret's School had always found the ceremony very funny.

On the Saturday before Easter, the last day of Lent, Lucy sat next to the center aisle for the ceremonial procession to the altar. When Gabriel passed by, carrying the tall lighted candle, she could easily have reached out and touched the starched white sleeve of his robe.

At noon Lent was officially over. There'd been

no word from Gabriel. Jeanie begged Lucy to go with her to the Arc that afternoon. "It'll be such fun! Everybody will be there!" Lucy wanted to go even more than Jeanie did, and changed her mind several times before finally deciding to stay at home. It was true that everyone went to the movies on this special Saturday, no matter what was playing, because it was the end of Lent. But if she came in with Jeanie, it would be a reminder that Gabriel hadn't kept his promise.

17

Lucy rang the doorbell of the Mother House of the Daughters of Mary in Ottawa. She'd been disappointed to learn that she was staying in a convent and not with a family, as the regional candidates had when they had come to Rockford. This would probably feel like sleeping in a haunted house. Still, she told herself, it would be something to tell Gabriel when she saw him again.

But instead of the narrow, windowless nun's cell that she'd been dreading, Lucy was shown into a large, sunny bedroom on the second floor. "This room is Carmelia's, one of our boarders

208

from the university," said Sister Ursula, the stern nun who had answered the door. "Carmelia has gone home to Brazil for the Easter vacation and charitably offered her room for your use."

"Thank you," Lucy said, speaking to the absent owner. She looked around, trying not to show her amazement at the elegant clothes cupboard with its full-length mirror, the giant pink stuffed dog on the bed, and the sparkling row of perfume and nail-polish bottles on the dressing table.

"There isn't much room left, but I assume you won't be needing space for . . . ?" Sister Ursula waved her pale hand over the dressing table, as if to sweep it clear.

Lucy shook her head.

"As a true scholar, you do not burden yourself with such objects of vanity," the nun said, pointing to the plain black suitcase that had been Tessa's when she went to convent school. "Have you considered a vocation in the religious life?"

"No, Sister," Lucy answered, borrowing confidence from Carmelia, who had dared to take makeup and a ridiculous toy dog inside a convent.

On her way out the nun turned in the doorway. "I understand that you possess a fine intellect," she said, her mouth drooping sadly as though she'd mentioned a serious flaw. "You might consider following the example of our beloved Sister Andrew."

As soon as the door closed and she was alone, Lucy hugged herself from pleasure at the beautiful room. She took her velvet dress from Tessa's suitcase and hung it up in the packed, perfumed closet, then opened the room door. All the rooms along the passage had been closed when she had come in. But now the door across the passage was wide open. She could see a young woman sitting cross-legged on the bed. She was wearing yellow pajamas and glasses with thick dark frames. The bed was covered with so many papers and books that some had slid to the floor.

Lucy was about to move back and close her own door when she heard herself called: "Hello, Lucy!" The girl slid carefully off the bed, picked up some of the papers from the floor, and carried them in her arms to the doorway. "I know who you are because Sister Andrew was one of my professors. My name is Philippa, but everybody calls me Phil." She leaned forward and looked down the long, silent hall. "You and I are the only ones here right now, so come on in if you get lonesome, or if you need space to hang your clothes."

The closet door was open, and Lucy could see

that it was almost empty, although every flat surface in the room was covered with books.

"I'm working on my thesis," Phil said. "That's
why I'm back early from vacation."

"I didn't mean to interrupt you," Lucy said
shyly.

Phil laughed. "I like an excuse to stop, and having another civilian around. Why don't you come
in and share some sinful chocolate-covered bis-
cuits I just brought from home?"

After Lucy went to bed, she lay awake for a
long time. She had undressed quickly, hoping to
fall asleep before she started thinking of the
exams tomorrow. She'd never met anyone like
Phil, but she liked her already. Victor would probably have liked her too. She'd once heard him
try to convince Edward after a movie they'd all
seen together that the actress who had played the
heroine's best friend was actually more attractive
because she was smarter, and funnier, and more
interesting.

The best friend had been less pretty. She'd
worn glasses in dark, heavy frames and clothes
that were very plain, just like Phil's. But Lucy liked
the way Phil looked. Although her hair was
straight and brown, like Lucy's, it was brushed

smooth, so instead of just hanging down, it swung forward at an angle across her cheek. When Phil was talking, she had a habit of moving her head to one side and flicking the shiny curtain of hair back and away from her face, like a pony tossing its mane.

Lucy moved her head sideways against the pillow and wondered if she might learn to flip her hair back too, in that interesting way, before she returned to Saint Margaret's.

When Lucy went into the bathroom the next morning, Phil was brushing her teeth at one of a long row of sparkling washbasins. She smiled at Lucy in the mirror. "What time will you be free today, Lucy?"

Lucy had slept badly in the silence of the convent. She didn't want to think of the day ahead. "About four o'clock," she answered glumly.

"I thought I'd show you around the university before supper."

Lucy looked around at the gray walls and white ceilings, the perfectly polished gray floor, and shivered. She wondered if Claire was still thinking of becoming a nun. She ought to tell Phil the truth, that she'd be wasting her time showing her a university.

"Doesn't it feel strange to live in a convent like

this?" she asked. "It isn't anything like a place where people live, is it? Even the dining room has stained-glass windows."

"It *does* feel a little like you're eating your poached egg in church," Phil said, laughing.

For the essay Lucy had to describe something she'd done that she'd been afraid to do. She'd been afraid of going inside the convent in Rockford that first time, but the judges would probably consider that not a proper subject to write about. She'd been even more afraid when she had finally asked Papa for a New Year's Day blessing. She'd never done it before, even though the nuns always reminded their classes before each Christmas vacation. She just couldn't imagine Papa making the sign of the cross over her head, like a priest. She hadn't even known whether asking him would make him angry, or make him laugh.

But last year, in the seventh grade, Sister Rose had announced that a trophy would be awarded to the class with the highest percentage of students who had received their fathers' blessings on New Year's Day. Lucy hadn't wanted her class to lose on her account, and so right after breakfast on New Year's morning she'd said to Jeanie, "Come with me." Jeanie had followed her to the living room, where Papa was, without asking a lot of questions first for a change. And when Lucy knelt down next to Papa's chair, Jeanie did the same, still without saying a word.

Papa was reading the newspaper, and didn't realize they were there until Lucy said, "Papa, please give us your blessing for the New Year." He put the paper down and looked at Lucy for such a long time and with such a serious expression in his eyes that she thought her request had made him angry, or worse, that it had hurt his feelings. But Papa reached out, put his hands on either side of her face, and pulled her toward him. He kissed her forehead, not right in the middle, but over to one side. Then he kissed Jeanie. Lucy waited for him to make the sign of the cross over their heads, but he just pulled Jeanie onto his lap and hugged them both together, very tightly.

Luckily, Jeanie didn't tell anyone at school that Papa had only kissed them. Lucy was sure the nuns would say that a kiss didn't count as a proper blessing. But she couldn't have asked Papa to make the sign of the cross when he had seemed so sure the blessing was over, and especially after he said to Lucy over the top of Jeanie's head, "My father did this when I was a boy. I didn't know it was still done." Lucy hadn't been able to say anything after that.

Lucy filled a page with rough notes, then crumpled it up. The sudden noise made several heads turn in her direction. She'd have to start over, but she couldn't write about Papa for an essay competition. Of course, she hadn't known it would turn out to be his very last New Year's Day, but whenever she thought of it afterward, she wished she hadn't asked for his blessing. It seemed that in some way she'd helped God decide that Papa's life was complete, that it was time to end it.

Without making notes, Lucy wrote a long description of the time she'd been afraid to skate on Griffith Lake after it froze during the night one Halloween. The lake's rough surface had been transformed into mile after mile of perfectly smooth, solid ice. There was no way of telling how thick the ice was, and it wasn't until she'd seen hundreds of people excitedly walking and skating all over the lake, some of them almost disappearing into the distance, that Lucy felt it was probably safe.

She'd skated all day until long after dark, stopping only to warm herself at one of the huge bonfires along the shoreline. But that night she dreamed she'd fallen through the ice and was trapped in the water underneath. A crowd of people was standing above her, looking down through the ice. She could see the zigzag patterns on the soles of their snow boots and the kind, worried expressions on their faces, but they watched her calmly, without moving to help.

Lucy described the sudden transformation of the lake and the dreamlike freedom of skating on such an endless expanse of ice. She thought of cutting out the part about the actual dream, then decided to leave it in when she remembered that the essay was supposed to be about fear. All that day, while she skated, she really had been afraid that she might fall through the ice.

It was late afternoon by the time Lucy and Phil arrived at the university. The setting sun threw shafts of golden light between the buildings. Some of the buildings were very old, with shadowy passageways and high, narrow windows that were pointed at the top, like the windows in a church. Others were new, with flat glass walls that reflected the bright-blue sky and the clouds.

Lucy stopped to watch a fountain, a silvery-blue column of water that climbed upward into the sunlight. When it reached the top, the water fell back in a mist that formed a tiny, perfect rainbow. She wished Jeanie could see the fountain and its rainbow, and the flower bed filled with thousands of red and yellow tulips.

When the tour was over, Lucy was glad that Phil hadn't asked her what she thought. She didn't want to pretend that she was hoping to be a student too one day at a place like this. As they sat on the bench waiting to take the bus back to the convent, a young man and woman came and stood next to them. They seemed to be waiting for the bus too, but it was hard to tell because he had his back to the street and both his hands were leaning flat against a tree trunk. The woman was standing inside his arms, facing him. They were talking in very low voices, with their faces close together.

Lucy had been watching the couple for a while before she realized that Phil was looking at her. "Are those people students at the university?" Lucy asked.

"Probably," Phil said. She looked at the couple, then at Lucy. "Are you thinking that might be you someday?"

Lucy felt her face turn hot, but forced herself to watch the couple a moment longer. "I won't be going to a university," she said.

Phil's smile vanished, but she went on looking at Lucy. "Someday you'll be a very handsome woman, Lucy."

"Handsome," Lucy repeated. "That's what people call you when they think you're not pretty or even good-looking."

Phil laughed. "Almost nobody is pretty, haven't

you noticed?" she said. Lucy couldn't tell if Phil really believed that.

Phil reached over and pushed Lucy's hair back behind her ears, then looked at her. "All you need is a good haircut," she said. "You have nice ears. You should show them off instead of hiding them."

Lucy stood up. The bus had arrived in a cloud of noise and smoke. "Nobody looks at ears," she said, and hurried onto the bus ahead of Phil.

Lucy took a window seat and looked out. The street was filled with people she didn't know. She'd almost decided earlier to tell Phil about Gabriel and ask her for advice on how to act and what to say the next time she saw him at school. But she was very tired now, and so confused that she didn't know how to start.

On Sunday morning Lucy took the train back to Rockford. The results of the final exams had been announced the night before. She'd received an honorable mention for essay writing, an elegant certificate that had been wrapped around her essay to form a scroll and tied with red ribbon. Scott had received three third prizes, but hadn't even come close to winning the boys' scholarship. He had cried after the announcements, sitting across the aisle from Lucy with his mother, who tried to console him.

Lucy didn't cry, but she was surprised at how disappointed she felt and how hard it had been to say good-bye to Phil. She hadn't wanted to give up Carmelia's beautiful room. It was the kind of room she could have had by winning that scholarship and going on later to a university.

When Lucy arrived at school the next day, Jeanie ran up to meet her. "Old Lima Bean wants to see you right away!" she said breathlessly.

"Don't worry," Lucy said calmly. But she dreaded having to see Sister Rose, whatever the reason.

Lucy knocked on the door of Sister Rose's office. There was no answer, so she went up the stairs to the second floor. The door to the nuns' study was open, and Sister Rose was standing next to the long polished table. Only the pictures and the lamp, with its comforting light, were gone, but the room seemed strange, and empty.

"I wanted to welcome you back," Sister Rose said, holding out a white envelope. Lucy took it and opened the stiff flap. Inside was a gold-edged bookmark with a picture of Saint Francis preaching to small animals and birds. From the top of the bookmark hung a loop of knotted brown cord with a heavy tassel on the end, like a monk's belt. Lucy drew the silky tassel through her fingers and said, "Thank you, Sister."

"We are all grateful to you," Sister Rose said. "You've set a fine example for others to follow."

"Thank you, Sister," Lucy said again, and turned to leave. She'd give the bookmark to Jeanie, she decided. She didn't want to be rewarded as if she'd really tried to do something for Saint Margaret's.

After supper, while they were still putting away the clean dishes, Lucy offered the bookmark to Jeanie, who accepted delightedly. "Being in that play was the most fun I've ever had," she said, gazing with a dreamy smile at the picture of St. Francis, "especially the night you won all those prizes. And Gabriel was so nice to me the whole time. I wish he hadn't moved away."

"Moved away?" Lucy had to force the words through the tight pain in her throat, so her voice sounded oddly deep. "Where?"

"Didn't you hear? He moved to Montreal," Jeanie said. Lucy couldn't speak, and after a silence Jeanie let out a long sigh. "He was my father, you know, in the play I mean," she said. "But the rest of the time he was like a very nice big brother."

Lucy stared straight ahead at the cupboard shelf. "Gabriel was *not* your father," she said angrily, her voice high and shrill. "And he wasn't your brother either!" Alarmed, Jeanie let the bookmark slip from her fingers as Lucy ran from the kitchen, her face wet with sudden, uncontrollable tears.

18

THE SUN HAD SET on the opposite side of the house before Lucy could stop herself from crying. She lifted her head and looked out the attic landing window at the shadows slowly lengthening across the yard. In the distance the rocks seemed to be sinking into a soft, dark sea.

A group of boys carrying kites appeared, on a high, flat rock. As there was no room to run and launch the kites, they had to toss them into the air to catch the wind. At first the kites just tumbled back down, but as soon as one caught the wind, it climbed so fast that it seemed suddenly free from its strings and from the earth's gravity. Before long all the kites were specks of color afloat in the sky, and the boys stood in shadow, like gray statues with hands outstretched, their faces turned upward. Above them in the round, wide sky the kites nodded as if they were alive.

By the time the boys brought the kites down, it was almost dark; but as they were leaving, another boy arrived with a kite that Lucy could barely see. Its gray shape rose slowly, stalled, then rose a little farther and disappeared. Lucy was still watching the place where the kite had disappeared when it reappeared suddenly, much higher, glowing red-gold, as if it had caught fire. It had climbed into the light where the sun still shone from below the horizon. The kite swayed from side to side, as if saying "No," then dropped back into shadow and vanished.

Lucy felt something warm creeping down her cheeks. Without knowing it she'd started to cry again. The thick, hot tears were as surprising and magical as the kite's sudden reappearance in light that she hadn't known was there. In her lap was an old notebook that she'd found among Victor's books in the attic. Its pages were covered with Victor's handwriting—stories and poems that he'd copied, some notes from his classes, and here and there, printed in the margins, girls' names that Lucy didn't recognize. Lucy turned to a blank page and started writing.

From then on she wrote every evening in Victor's notebook, which she kept in the box where she'd found it. Each time she wrote, it was as though a hand had lifted a round stone inside her and relieved her for a moment of its weight.

Sometimes she copied out words from Victor's textbooks, especially the ones he had marked, such as the line from a poem: "Therefore all seasons shall be sweet to thee." She'd tried repeating the line out loud, to see if it would help her remember what Victor's voice sounded like. She couldn't remember.

She never wrote about Gabriel. Once she'd forced herself to admit that she'd never see him again, the thought was a dark, shifting numbness that accompanied her everywhere, like a shadow on the inside.

She had to stay after school for a while to catch up on her math, and she'd given Sister Andrew the essay she'd written for the finals, still wrapped in its certificate and red ribbon. But when the school year finally ended, Lucy walked out through Saint Margaret's front door with the feeling that a snake must have, she wrote later in

Victor's notebook, when it slips out of its old skin.

The house had never been so empty and quiet. Tessa's husband, Leo, had finally found a job in British Columbia and sent for Tessa and the twins. Mr. Porter had married very quietly, and to everyone's surprise, and moved out too. Mama decided not to rent out his room again until September, and moved into it with Jeanie. Lucy had their old room to herself for the summer.

Before leaving, Tessa arranged for Lucy to have her hair cut for free by an expert who was coming to Rockford to demonstrate the latest hairstyles. On a hot Sunday afternoon in late June Lucy sat in a raised chair in front of a room full of people while a strange man brushed her hair forward over her face. She heard the scissors and saw thick pieces of her hair fall like soft animal fur around the man's feet.

When he held a mirror in front of Lucy, the first thing she saw was the shocked look on her own face. Her hair was almost all gone. What was left looked like a smooth cap with only a few, slightly longer, wisps of hair behind her ears and across her forehead.

"Are you trying to be one of the boys now?" Edward asked when he saw her. Having checked her reflection in every store window she passed, Lucy had to admit she didn't look much like a girl. But after a few days she decided that she liked having her hair so short, because it made her head feel wonderfully light and cool.

Alice was away at dance camp. Claire had come back to Saint Margaret's several times during the last two or three weeks of school, but she'd always arrived just as class was letting out, and talked with Lucy only for a few minutes while she waited to see Sister Andrew. Without her front teeth, Claire's face had looked collapsed and old. If someone walked by while she and Lucy were talking, she turned her face to the wall. On the last day of school Claire had told Lucy that an aunt was coming to take care of her mother and her brothers and sisters, and that she was moving to a cottage on the lake for the summer to help Mrs. Precious, who was expecting a baby.

Lucy was sewing a pleated green-and-blue-tartan skirt for high school. Mama had helped her measure and pin the fabric so that the pleats would be green on the outside and blue on the inside. But it was so hot, even in the morning, that the wool cloth made Lucy's fingers sweat and itch. When she made a mistake, all the pleats she'd made from then on had to be unpinned, pressed out, and measured again. After a few days she gave up and spent time in her room instead, reading and writing.

One blazing hot afternoon when Lucy was on her way home from an errand for Mama, she heard her name called. She recognized Claire's voice—otherwise she'd never have suspected that the girl running and waving from the other side of the street was Claire. She was wearing white sandals and a white summer dress that tied in soft bows at the shoulders. The dress had a full skirt that bounced as Claire ran across the street toward Lucy. The soft bows fluttered against Claire's neck when she turned her head to dodge the moving cars. As Lucy waited for Claire to cross the street, she was aware of her own rumpled summer shorts and halter top.

"You're not spending the summer at the lake?" Lucy asked.

"I am, but I come into town almost every day."

Claire's hair was still uneven, but it had grown out enough to comb smoothly to one side. It was fastened with a red hair clip in the shape of a heart. Claire was carrying books, which she shifted onto her other arm. Lucy pointed to them. "I'll walk with you to the library."

Claire laughed and held the books out to show

them to Lucy. "These aren't library books. They're for my classes at Rockford High."

"You're going to Rockford High?" Lucy's mouth was suddenly dry.

"Mrs. Precious thought of it first," Claire said, fanning herself with one of the books. "I didn't even know they had summer classes at R.H.S."

"R.H.S.?"

"Rockford High School. But it was Sister Andrew who talked the principal into accepting me. I was in his office and he was right in the middle of telling me all the reasons why he couldn't when the telephone rang. 'I fully agree, Sister,' and 'It's an honor to speak with you.'" Claire's imitation made Lucy laugh. "He seemed to recognize right away who Sister Andrew was. As soon as he hung up, he gave me some forms and explained how to enroll in summer classes. He called me 'Miss Durant'! I thought about you just then, Lucy."

"Why?"

"Because I knew Sister Andrew must be very famous, and she picked *you* to represent Saint Margaret's in the competition. That was quite an honor, don't you think?"

The hot sidewalk felt like a stovetop. Lucy moved onto the grass. "How can you be going to high school when you haven't finished the eighth grade?"

Claire moved to stand next to Lucy. "I know I didn't finish," she said, her voice low and close to anger. "That's why I'm with all the ninth-grade dummies who didn't pass some of their classes last year and have to take them again. I'm taking the classes for the first time, so I know even less than they do. I think they like having somebody like that around."

They'd both been watching the traffic. When they turned and looked at each other, they burst out laughing. Then Lucy saw the most startling change of all, the one she ought to have noticed from the first. Claire had teeth—not the usual, dead-looking kind of false teeth she'd seen before on old people, but a little uneven, exactly like real ones.

"At least I know my way around the school now, and some of the teachers," Claire said.

"And they let you dress like that?"

"Wouldn't Old Lima Bean have a fit?" Claire said, looking down at her own bare shoulders.

"I guess you've changed your mind about being a nun," Lucy said.

Claire sighed. "That was just an idea I had for a while. I have to go now."

Lucy watched as Claire ran quickly across the street, then turned to shout over the traffic before going on. "I'll call you just as soon as school's out!" Lucy nodded and waved back. In a moment the white dress was a floating, shimmering blur in the distance.

Lucy started to walk home through the stifling heat. Claire hadn't really changed. She was still the same, but she'd had to be smarter than even Lucy had realized to come from so far behind and end up in Rockford High before anyone else in their class. Claire wouldn't have sat day after day in Saint Margaret's Church, lost in dreams. But if she had, and heard noises, she would have gone to the basement to see what they were. If she'd been Lucy, Claire would have known that Gabriel was rehearsing a play with her own little sister. And she would have known that he was moving away.

When Lucy got home, she went to her room. She found some clean, blank sheets from Victor's notebook and started to write. She wrote rapidly, filling page after page, until her wrist and fingers were too cramped to go on.

In the late afternoon she went back, reread what she'd written, and made some changes. She recopied it neatly and, after trying unsuccessfully to think of a better title, wrote at the top of the first page, "Papa's New Year Blessing." She folded the papers neatly and slipped them into an envelope she addressed to Sister Andrew. She ran downstairs for some stamps, then out to the corner mailbox, and pushed the envelope inside before she could change her mind.

The days passed quickly from then on. Lucy filled all the blank pages in Victor's notebook and bought herself a new one. Jeanie wandered in often, looking lost in the quiet, empty house, and in the afternoons Lucy took her swimming or berry picking.

One morning Lucy was reading in her room when Alice suddenly appeared in the doorway. Her arms and legs were tanned, and she looked prettier than ever.

"How was dance camp?" Lucy asked, dazzled.

Alice sank onto Lucy's bed and let herself drop backward. "Too few boys and not enough to eat!" she groaned, then propped herself up on her elbows and looked around the room. Lucy had turned all the way around in her chair, but she was still sitting at the small, plain desk that Mr. Porter had left for her. "It's nice that you finally have a place to yourself," Alice said, "but isn't this an awful lot like that nuns' study you complained so much about?"

"I suppose it is," Lucy said, laughing.

Alice had picked up the statue of the Virgin from Lucy's bedside table when Mama called up the stairs, "Lucy! There's a telephone call for you!"

"Lucy? It's Claire!" Claire sounded happy and very excited. "Summer school is over, and Mrs. Precious gave me the day off to celebrate. She also gave me a new swimsuit, and I was wondering if you'd like to go to the lake with me. I'm going back home in a couple of days, so this might be my only chance."

To her own surprise Lucy heard herself say just as excitedly, "My friend Alice is here. Can she come too?"

"Sure!"

Lucy was in the kitchen making sandwiches to take to the lake when Claire arrived. Alice answered the front door. "What a nice beach bag!" Lucy heard her say.

"It's a gift from the woman I work for," Claire explained, "for passing all my summer classes."

By the time they came into the kitchen only a moment later, Claire and Alice were so deep in conversation that Lucy smiled when she looked up and saw them. Once, it seemed a very long time ago, she'd actually worried what would happen when Claire and Alice finally met. Now, miraculously and suddenly, they were both here in her house and as much at ease with each other as though they'd been together before on hundreds of other bright summer mornings.

At the lake they all swam and played in the water until they were exhausted, then stretched out in the sun on a flat rock that sloped gently into the water. Before long Alice was sitting up and looking out at the lake. Whenever a boat or canoe passed close by with boys in it, Alice described them in a low voice to Lucy and Claire.

Claire turned her face toward Lucy and said sleepily, "Lucy, your hair is already dry."

Alice reached back and lifted some of Lucy's hair with her fingers. "It falls right back into place," she said admiringly. "Did you know that your haircut is the latest style from France? It's called the 'gamin cut.'"

"I suppose you learned that in dance camp too," Lucy teased, and placed her bare foot against Alice's back, as if to push her into the water.

"No, I learned it in French class. It means 'little boy.' But the two of you know that already, don't you?"

"We know that word," Claire said, "but nobody we know ever uses it."

"So what do you say when you want to say 'little boy' in French?"

"We say 'little boy' in French," Lucy laughed, and gave Alice's back a much harder shove with her foot.

Alice was letting herself roll toward the water's edge; then she stopped and sat up very straight. "There's three boys out there in a canoe," she whispered dramatically. "They've been watching us, and now they're coming this way." She giggled softly. "One has nice curly hair. I saw him first, don't forget!"

Claire and Lucy both sat up quickly. "Don't move!" Alice whispered. Lucy lay down again, closed her eyes, and listened to the splash of paddles approaching. She wanted to stand up and run, but her back felt glued to the rough surface of the rock. She opened her eyes just enough to see that Claire and Alice were leaning their heads together. "Do you think they know we've been watching them?" she heard Claire ask, holding her breath.

"Alice was the only one watching them," Lucy said loudly, in a normal voice.

"Shhhh!" both girls said at once. Lucy raised her head just in time to see a canoe glide smoothly toward the rock. Two of the boys were holding dripping paddles across their knees. The third, the one with curly hair, sat between them, on the floor of the canoe.

They looked at least eighteen, maybe older—Lucy couldn't tell for sure. They were very tanned, so even though their faces were in shadow, she could tell that they were smiling.

Lucy closed her eyes and put her head back down. "Don't talk to them," she whispered frantically. "Tell them to go away! Please!" Her wet towel was cold and clammy, and she started to shiver uncontrollably.

"How can we tell them to go away if we don't talk to them?" Claire asked calmly, without turning around.

"You girls from around here?" asked a deep voice.

"Us girls are from around here," Alice answered, imitating the man's slow, flat accent.

Lucy heard Claire's soft laughter.

Alice turned and whispered fiercely to Lucy, "If you're so scared, just pretend you're sleeping and let us handle this."

There was a bumping, then a scraping against the rock.

"We're from Cleveland, Ohio. Know where that is?"

"Sure I know where that is. We learn all about you Yanks in school, don't we?" Alice must have looked at Claire just then, Lucy thought. "Even if you don't know anything about us."

"Come on, don't be like that," said another voice.

The canoe scraped the rock again. Lucy suddenly remembered that her feet were very close to the water's edge, but she couldn't move to pull them away.

"Don't come any closer, or you'll wake up our friend," Claire said.

"Claire! Alice! Stop! Please!" Lucy begged in a loud whisper. She was shivering so hard now that she started to laugh.

"From back there it was hard to tell if that was a girl or a boy, or what."

"Well, she isn't a what," Claire said.

Lucy was shaking hard with laughter.

"Why is her hair cut so short?"

"Because she's going to be a nun," Alice said.

"Alice!" Lucy and Claire said at the same time. There was a silence, then the sound of paddles splashing. "Are they leaving?" Lucy asked, not daring to look.

"They're going," Alice said. "Your hair scared them off." By the time Lucy was able to look, the canoe was already rounding the tree-covered rock point and was almost out of sight.

Now Claire and Alice were laughing uncontrollably. Lucy started to join in, but her stomach and sides were too sore and she was too weak from shivering to do anything other than curl up on her side. Alice and Claire, still laughing, collapsed together, then fell over in a heap on top of her.

That night Mama made blueberry shortcake with whipped cream for dessert. Lucy ate two helpings, and competed with Edward to see whose tongue was darker blue until Mama made them stop. "Go outside," she said. "You too, Jeanie. I'd rather wash the dishes myself than have all of you in here acting so silly in this heat."

They'd eaten supper late, so when they went outside, it was almost dark. They lay on the grass and looked up at the sky. The house blotted out part of the sky and made the stars that had already come out seem even brighter.

That afternoon, while Lucy was at the lake, Mama had finished her pleated skirt. She'd found it in her room and tried it on. Each pleat hung perfectly straight except those she'd made herself, but Mama had pressed them flat so that the unevenness hardly showed. When she moved, the pleats opened and closed exactly as they were supposed to. Lucy could hardly wait for school to start.

"I just remembered," Edward said. "There was

a telephone call for you from the convent. Sister Rose wants to see you."

Jeanie sat up. "Why does Old Lima Bean want to see Lucy?"

"She didn't say. She said it was about 'an unfinished matter.' "

"What unfinished matter?" Jeanie asked anxiously.

"I don't know," Edward said. "Maybe Lucy has to go to Saint Margaret's a while longer." He pushed her shoulder with his fist, but she didn't respond.

Today, Lucy realized for the first time, she'd been completely free of Saint Margaret's School and of everything that had happened to her there in those last months. But before she'd even had a chance to know that she *was* free, she'd already been called to go back.

19

Lucy searched among the clothes that Tessa had left behind for something to wear to the convent and decided on a flowered skirt and a white blouse that Mama had starched and ironed. With her hair as short as a boy's, Lucy looked out of place in the blouse, which had long, full sleeves and a deep frill edged with lace at the neck and wrists, but she didn't care. She was too worried about the reason she'd been called to the convent.

The convent was even smaller, more silent, and more closed in than she remembered. The lawn and the green hedge across the front were trimmed with perfectly straight edges, as usual. Unlike the houses all around it, the convent had no colorful flower beds, only two snowball bushes, one on each side of the front door. Lucy went up the steps feeling that something especially awful was about to happen.

The same little nun answered the door, pointed to the empty music room, then vanished inside the convent. The lid of the piano was closed. The bench that Mother Augusta had sat on had been pushed all the way underneath the piano, so there was no place to sit.

Lucy heard the whisper of moving cloth. Sister Andrew appeared in the doorway carrying some official-looking papers. A trickle of sweat ran down Lucy's back, under Tessa's blouse.

Sister Andrew looked at Lucy for a long time. "I see you've recovered your health after the ordeals of last spring?"

"Yes, thank you, Sister," Lucy said hoarsely, her eyes on the papers in Sister Andrew's hands.

"Something important has happened," Sister Andrew began. She paused and looked at Lucy.

Whatever had happened, Lucy thought, it must be so bad that Sister Andrew had to search for the right words to say what it was. "What's wrong?" Lucy asked finally.

Sister Andrew laughed, throwing her head back. "Nothing's wrong! Unless of course you choose to ignore your own good fortune, as you are wont to do. I showed your story to the editor of a scholastic journal. She wants to publish it, but she needs your permission."

"Someone wants to publish Papa's story?"

"*Your* story," Sister Andrew corrected. She unfolded the papers. "They want to call it 'The New Year's Blessing,'" if that meets with your approval. Take this form home and read it before signing. They also require your mother's signature. I'm sure she'll be proud of you." She paused. "I know I'm *very* proud of you," she said, extending her hand.

A moment later Lucy was outside the convent door. Sister Andrew's fingers had felt cool and dry, like chalk, even on such a hot day. Lucy touched one of the white puffs on the snowball bush. The cluster of tiny flowers released a perfume of such sweetness that her numbness dissolved. Everything came into clear, sharp focus: the intense green of the lawn and hedge, the steeple of Saint Margaret's Church.

She saw her story printed in hundreds, maybe thousands of copies. Strangers would read what she'd written about Papa. Lucy turned toward the door in panic. "I don't want what I wrote about my father to be given to strangers to read," she'd tell Sister Andrew.

Lucy turned back and ran down the convent steps. A moment later she was standing in front of the church and looking down at Saint Margaret's School. One hand was inside the pocket of Tessa's skirt holding the paper Sister Andrew had given her to sign. Under the summer sun the dusty school yard and chalk-stained walls seemed even shabbier than she remembered. Without their colored-paper decorations the windows looked lonely, like those of an abandoned building. But in the windows of the eighth-grade classroom the geranium plants had climbed high into a wild tangle. The giant leaves and clusters of red flowers looked unreal, like the ones Sister Isabel had once allowed her students to paint with their fingers, right on the glass. Someone had been watering the geranium pots all this time—probably Laurence Constantine, who had finally graduated and been hired to work for the school during the summer.

Lucy started to leave by walking carefully along the lowest of the granite steps leading up to the church. In the sunlight the cut stone sparkled under her feet, like snowflakes. Just as she reached the end, she heard someone call, "Hey, Lucy! Wait!" The voice was deep, like a man's, and had come from the school yard below. Laurence must have seen her just then, when she'd been thinking about him.

When Lucy glanced back, she saw Gabriel jump onto the far end of the step. He raised both arms and started walking along the step, placing one foot in front of the other, like a tightrope walker. He seemed afloat on the stone's shimmering light, like a heat mirage.

Lucy watched Gabriel approaching, her hands clenched inside the pockets of Tessa's skirt to steady herself. When he'd almost reached her, his foot slipped off the edge of the step. Lucy's hands flew up to catch him, but he didn't fall, and she quickly put them back in her pockets. Her fingers touched the folded paper.

Gabriel was standing in front of her now. "I wasn't sure it was you at first," he said, pointing shyly at her hair. "It's nice."

Lucy's head felt unbearably hot. Her knees and ankles seemed ready to melt. She suddenly realized that she was staring at Gabriel and looked quickly to the side, toward Saint Margaret's School.

"What are you doing here?" she asked finally, and immediately regretted the question. It sounded rude.

"My father had to come back to Rockford on

business. I asked to come with him," Gabriel said. "I went to see Sister Andrew, and she told me you'd be coming to the convent today. Is anything wrong?"

"It's about a story I wrote. It's . . . They're going to publish it." She'd blurted it out all wrong, unable to raise her head.

"I knew it!" Gabriel shouted.

Lucy looked up. He seemed nervous, as though in a hurry to go someplace else, probably Madeleine's. "Well, I just wanted to tell somebody," she said with forced cheerfulness, backing away.

"Please don't go yet. I wanted to give you this," Gabriel said, holding out his hand. On it was a shining gold circle. "It's a bracelet, and this is called a charm."

"I know," Lucy said, picking up the charm and turning it carefully in her fingers. "A book," she whispered, hardly breathing.

Gabriel laughed. "Maybe it's your story."

"But you didn't know—" Lucy dropped the tiny gold book as though it had burned her fingers. "It's another joke, isn't it? It's not really for me!" She turned away blindly, and stepped off the edge onto empty air. She regained her balance and stumbled forward. She rounded the corner of the church and broke into a run.

When she reached the cemetery faucet, she took hold of it with both hands and sank to her knees on the ground, rocking back and forth to keep herself from crying. Her hands turned the water on and off, so a pool of mud formed under her knees. With her head down Lucy saw only the huge wet flowers of Tessa's skirt. They looked monstrous, like flowers in a nightmare.

Her heart was being squeezed tightly, as if by a giant fist. Papa had died of something called "heart seizure." It must have felt like this, only much worse. But she couldn't imagine anything worse.

Lucy sat back on her heels and took a deep breath.

She felt a hand on her shoulder. Gabriel had followed her. She lifted her head and saw him slip the gold bracelet into his pocket.

"I was thirsty," she said. She stood up and brushed off the grass and mud. "But there's nothing here to drink from." She felt ridiculous.

Gabriel leaned over, turned on the faucet, and cupped both his hands under it. He stood up slowly, water trickling between his fingers. "Hurry up before it's all gone!"

Lucy bent down and tried to drink, but she started to laugh and the water choked her. Suddenly Gabriel's cupped hands were gone and she felt their cool, damp weight on her shoulders, pulling her toward him. Her eyes blinked shut in surprise, and Gabriel's mouth, warm and velvety, pressed against hers.

Gabriel let go and Lucy stepped back. The cemetery was a blur of green with bright-yellow patches where the sun shone through the leaves and red, blue, and pink where flowers stood on the graves. Her face was hot and prickly.

"The bracelet really was for you," Gabriel said. "To let you know I was sorry."

"About what?" Gabriel didn't answer. "Sorry about what?" Lucy asked again.

After a long, deep sigh Gabriel looked straight into her eyes and said, "When I saw you just now, I almost didn't call to you."

"Why not?"

"When I found out that my family was moving, I was going to ask you if we could write to each other." Gabriel's voice was strangely thick and the words had come in a rush. He paused.

"Why didn't you? You didn't even tell me you were leaving." Lucy stood so still, waiting for Gabriel's answer, that she heard a faint movement at her shoulders where the starched cloth was uncrinkling from the pressure of Gabriel's wet hands. The sleeves of Tessa's blouse felt like wings. "Why didn't you? I would have said yes."

Gabriel turned and frowned at Lucy. "Raymond told me about a toy ring he gave you as a joke, with a note that had my name on it," he said quickly. "He told me while we were sitting in front of the stage on the night of the announcements. He said he'd forgotten all about it. Then I saw you winning all those prizes, and I felt so stupid for telling you I'd take you to the movies if you won, as if *that* was some special prize." Gabriel sighed again, then took a deep breath before going on. "So I got up and left right away. I felt awful. After that I was glad we were moving far away."

Lucy wanted to tell Gabriel of her disappointment and how much she had wanted the special prize of going to the movies with him. But she had other prizes now, she realized with a jolt, a prize she'd given herself—"The New Year's Blessing"—and Sister Andrew's words, "I'm very proud of you."

"I *will* write to you if you still want me to," she said faintly.

"*Now* will you accept this?" Gabriel said, holding the bracelet out to her.

Lucy raised her left hand and let him slip the

bracelet over it. He bent over to fasten the clasp, and his hair almost touched her face. It smelled warm, like Min Min's fur.

Lucy let her hand drop. They looked at one another.

"My father will be waiting for me," Gabriel said at last.

"Should I tell you my address?"

"I already have it. Jeanie wrote it out for me. Will you say hello to her?"

"Yes." Lucy had started walking slowly backward.

Gabriel stood leaning against the faucet, watching her.

Lucy raised her left arm, as if to shield her eyes from a dazzling light. The tiny book hung trembling, like a golden water drop, at the corner of her vision. She turned and walked on faster, until she was running to keep herself from looking back.